A SURG

It was no wonder surgeons Nick Da Costa
and Felicity Meredith loathed each other
on sight! He thought she was just a cold-
blooded careerist, relying on her father's
reputation to get her where she wanted to
go. And she thought that Nick, in spite of
his too-good-to-be true looks and reputation, was prejudiced, chauvinistic and a
womaniser to boot!

A SURGEON SURRENDERS

BY

HOLLY NORTH

MILLS & BOON LIMITED
15–16 BROOK'S MEWS
LONDON W1A 1DR

First published in Great Britain 1985 by Mills & Boon Limited

© Holly North 1985

Australian copyright 1985 Philippine copyright 1985

ISBN 0 263 75235 6

Set in 10 on 12 pt Linotron Times
03–1185–52,000

Photoset by Rowland Phototypesetting Limited Bury St Edmunds, Suffolk Made and printed in Great Britain by Richard Clay (The Chaucer Press) Limited Bungay, Suffolk

CHAPTER ONE

'Oh lord, I'd forgotten we were due for an audience today!' Barney Morton, senior general surgeon at Highstead Hospital, rinsed his hands in approved fashion, running the water down from his wrists and off the end of his fingertips, and knocked the tap with his elbow.

'At least we've got something a bit out of the ordinary for them,' Felicity Meredith, his junior registrar, said lightly—or as lightly as she could, bearing in mind that she had been up since two this morning and had spent most of the intervening six hours worrying what to do about Mrs Vera Morrissey, the patient who was to be number one on the list. A dozen or so young student nurses had just come squeaking across the gleaming tiled floor and taken their positions well back from the operating table. They were exchanging nervous glances, and through the thick glass of the observation window of the scrub room, Fliss could hear Sister Tutor giving instructions and explaining what was what in the theatre.

Fliss dried her hands on the sterile towel laid out for her and cast a nervous glance of her own at Barney. With Mrs Morrissey suddenly crammed on to an already tight schedule, it was unlikely that he would be able to do his Cinderella act and disappear for his private work in good time. On Tuesdays Barney left at twelve; everyone knew that and was supposed to respect his divine right as senior registrar to vanish when he felt the urge. Private patients were not like NHS ones, he explained if anyone grumbled. And with four—or was it five? Fliss

wondered, confused—children to get into prep school
he needed the extra cash that a couple of afternoons a
week at a private clinic in Harrow could provide. Fliss
had half expected a rocket for not performing an emergency operation on Mrs Morrissey in the small hours
and so allowing him to get through this morning's list
on schedule.

But she disliked operating at a time when the metabol-
ism of both patient and surgeon was at its lowest ebb,
and she didn't really see why it was necessary for an
anaesthetist and the duty surgeon to have to leave their
beds just to make things a bit more convenient for Mr
Morton. So Mrs Morrissey had waited and, as it turned
out, Barney had sailed in in a genial mood. If only Fliss
didn't feel so completely exhausted, she might have had
it in her to be pleased. As it was, she stepped into her
surgical gown, snapped into her gloves and reflected, not
for the first time, on the tyranny that held sway over the
operating theatre. All through her studentship she had
thought that once she was a surgeon things would be
different; and now she was and they weren't. Juniors still
did all the slog and high-ups still stepped in and took the
glory.

Peter Locke, the team's anaesthetist and her friend of
some years, entered the theatre with Mrs Morrissey,
scarcely recognisable in the theatre gown and hat and
socks and with, no doubt, her false teeth tactfully removed. The student nurses fluttered visibly, though
whether with nerves at seeing the comatose patient or
with youthful feminine interest in Peter, Fliss wasn't
sure. Sister Tutor was giving general explanations about
the anaesthetic equipment and by his gestures Fliss
could see that he was telling everyone what he was
doing.

Sister McIlvaney, who ran the theatres as if they were a military training camp, was checking the sterile trays of instruments and arranging autoclaved drapes over vital portions of Mrs Morrissey's anatomy. At her side, Jenny Webster, who had joined the team two weeks ago and had hardly spoken since, so frightened was she of doing something wrong, counted up swabs and did the 'dirty' work.

'Ready?' Barney, at Fliss's side, strode out into the arena, timing his entrance perfectly. Having an audience didn't bother him in the slightest; he was always something of a showman, and adoring female eyes seemed to bring out his most extreme flamboyance. Fliss, on the other hand, found student days rather nerve-racking. She was a competent surgeon, she knew; but she didn't have that streak of egoism that allowed her to tell jokes while she was delving into someone's abdomen.

Sister McIlvaney greeted her idol—for she and Barney had both been here more than twenty years— and nodded to Fliss, so tall and slim, as she took her place across the table. Fliss glanced at Peter, but he seemed not to see her, though she was sure he was looking in her direction. He'd done that once or twice lately, she thought sharply; in fact she wasn't the only one who had noted that he wasn't his usual cheerful self. But she had no time to contemplate the matter.

'As it was Miss Meredith who was called out to see Mrs Morrissey at two this morning, perhaps she would like to explain what we're going to do now.'

A dozen sets of eyes swivelled above their masks to survey Highstead's lady surgeon, and Fliss felt desperately uncomfortable under the combined gaze. She knew she wasn't the glamorous figure that TV serials had led them to expect. She was tall and mousy and far too

busy to worry about her appearance—and very selfconscious. Somehow she felt a bit of a let-down. In all the
hospital stories she had read, Fliss had noted that lady
surgeons were supposed to have wild affairs with all the
handsome men they met over the operating table; they
were supposed to emerge from a day fiddling with tonsils
and gall bladders in a fit condition to go for candlelit
meals; they were supposed to have manes of Titian hair
that tumbled down their backs when they pulled off their
theatre caps and caused surgeons to gasp in amazement.

No one ever mentioned the problems of dry skin from
all that scrubbing with astringent lotions, or pasty faces
caused by the artificial lighting, or the fact that surgeons'
feet tended to spread a size from the simple fact of
standing still for so long, let alone the fact that it was
sometimes impossible to get the smell of ether and
formaldehyde out of your pores or stay awake after four
nights on duty . . .

'Mrs Morrissey had a major operation yesterday—a
gastric resection,' Fliss ventured in an unsure voice. 'The
operation went smoothly and she was returned to the
wards without any problem. But her blood pressure has
since remained low, despite the regular methods to bring
it up to normal, and I was called in this morning when
she began to vomit blood.' She cleared her throat and
thought how like a schoolteacher she sounded. 'Who
knows the correct term for this?'

A freckled girl standing next to Sister Tutor attracted
Fliss's attention with a nod, then replied efficiently,
'Haematemesis—the blood that is vomited looks like
coffee grounds because it has been partially digested.'

'That's right,' Fliss smiled. 'What we're pretty sure
has happened is that a blood vessel, quite a small one, is
haemorrhaging intra-gastrically. We'll reopen the

wound, checking for infection or other possible causes of the problem as we go, and secure the blood vessel when we find it.'

Sister McIlvaney whipped back the covering drape to expose Mrs Morrissey's bruised abdomen and the bright scar from yesterday's operation like a conjuror revealing a box of tricks. There was a concerted hiss of sharply indrawn breath from the collected students at the sight, then Sister swabbed with antiseptic and Barney checked with Peter that all was well enough for them to proceed.

'Fine,' he said coolly, 'though don't take too long. After yesterday I don't want to have to put her too far under.' He twiddled a knob theatrically, as if to underline his statement, and Fliss set to work, undoing the stitches she had so neatly closed up with less than twenty-four hours ago.

Everything continued in a routine manner, and when the gall bladder came into view Barney called the bravest of the students to have a look despite Peter's creased brow and Fliss's irritation at the encroaching hands of the clock. Sister McIlvaney watched such hoo-ha benevolently, reserving her blackest frown for the two nurses who declined the invitation for a detailed view of Mrs Morrissey's inner workings. If they didn't have the stomach for something like this, they would never make theatre nurses, in her opinion . . .

'Ah, now we're getting to the source of the problem,' Barney muttered, probing gently with his forceps while Fliss held back the layers of subcutaneous tissue with a retractor. 'If I just . . .'

A thin spurt of blood curved up from the wound and splashed the front of Fliss's theatre greens; a wild shriek went up from some of the students watching and there was a gentle crumpling sound, as of a large building delicately brought to the ground—or a nurse folding at the knees in a faint.

'*Haemostat,*' ordered Fliss, trying to ignore the hysterical giggles that seemed to have overcome the students. Sister McIlvaney, who after all these years in theatre was quite capable of performing an operation herself, had anticipated the request and banged a curved Kelly haemostat into Fliss's palm. Two seconds later and the blood vessel was secured and everyone around the table looked up to see what all the fuss was about.

Sister Tutor was trying to bring the girl who had passed out round, and several trainees were ranged along the back wall of the theatre, as if due for the firing squad—and indeed, from the beetling of Sister Tutor's brows, Fliss guessed that some of them might have preferred to face a firing squad rather than the scolding they were going to get any minute now!

'Och, a load of lily-livers, all of you!' Sister McIlvaney fumed as she aspirated the remaining blood.

Barney was the only one unperturbed by the incident. 'We'll need a diathermy set, Nurse,' he instructed Jenny. 'Now, who here can tell me what we use diathermy for?'

But there was no reply as Sister Tutor hustled her pupils from the theatre. Barney turned a genuinely bemused eye on Fliss. 'What on earth's all the fuss about?' he asked innocently.

'You look absolutely dreadful!' Fliss, with a forkful of hotpot halfway to her mouth, looked up to see the amused features of Kate Bailey above her.

'Thank you for those kind words,' she grinned, shifting her tray along the table to make room for the only other woman doctor in the hospital. 'And may I say that you're looking a little wan yourself?'

'You may. And I'm prepared to put money on the fact that you haven't earned those bags under your eyes by dancing the nights away with some gorgeous man.' Kate plumped herself down at Fliss's side and began sorting through her own portion of rapidly congealing stew. It was gone two and the senior staff canteen could not provide gourmet fare at the best of times; catch it after one and even the most robust appetites were faced with a challenge.

'This is my fifth and final night of standby duty,' Fliss concurred. 'How about you?' She knew all to well that Kate, as a junior doctor, was expected to work longer hours than most surgeons, particularly as Highstead's casualty department was strictly limited.

'Not too bad this week, so far, but I did ninety-eight hours last week and I'm still trying to recover. Do you ever wonder why you put up with it?'

'Sometimes—particularly when Barney dashes off to supplement his own income and leaves me with a bladder tear to do on my own,' Fliss admitted gloomily. 'And with Nigel away on honeymoon I'm having to do everything.' Nigel was the third member of Barney's team, the registrar. He and his wife, one of the administrators, were in the Bahamas for three weeks. Immediately Fliss felt churlish for begrudging them their trip.

'Honestly, these men!' Kate's face, usually so highly coloured but at the moment pale with weariness, lit up. 'They wouldn't have left you with all this work to do if you'd been a man—a man they'd respect more. You won't believe it, but I did a ward round with old Bennett this morning, and when we got back to the office he dismissed Sister and told me to go and get the coffee! He

wouldn't have dreamed of asking one of the male doctors to do it. And when I told him so he laughed and
made some sexist joke about how a little power turned
women's heads and made them think they were capable
of anything! I ask you!' she huffed, chucking her fork
back on to the plate.

Fliss smiled sympathetically. Kate was a feminist, one
of the militant variety who believed in confronting male
chauvinism when she met it. Fliss didn't have the courage to do that, though she had met plenty of prejudice in
her time; no, she preferred to show the male bastions of
the medical world how good she was by being better than
they were, which explained why she had progressed so
rapidly through the ranks to her present position—and
why she was feeling so exhausted. Just one word about
feeling overworked and, she knew, someone from one
of the other teams could come in to cover for her. But
her pride wouldn't even let her contemplate the idea.

'You should just have ignored him,' she said aloud.
'I'm sure he only does it to provoke you.'

Kate raised her eyebrow. 'I had my own back. I
sugared his coffee for him and sat stirring it for a very
long time. When he asked what I was doing, I said I was
only trying to make him feel at home—after all, didn't
his wife always stir his coffee for him, just like his mother
used to?'

'You didn't!'

'I did. He went rather pink and kept asking me
awkward questions about the most difficult cases.'

Fliss was still chuckling. 'It wasn't *that* funny,'
protested Kate, her dark brown eyes curious.

Fliss wiped a tear from her lashes. 'No,' she swallowed. 'It's just that I can imagine my father being
exactly the same.'

Sir Mortimer Meredith was a rather well-known eye surgeon; he now spent much of his time abroad, particularly in America, where the newest technology was assisting almost daily breakthroughs. And though he was her father and she loved him dearly, and though he was, everyone agreed, a great surgeon, no one, not even his nearest and dearest, could deny that he tended to be a bit pompous, especially in his hospital habitat, surrounded by admiring juniors.

'You should re-educate him, then,' Kate said sternly. 'Don't allow him to get away with it—at the breakfast table or anywhere.'

'He's not like it with me,' protested Fliss. 'He's always treated me just as he would a son, encouraged me . . . But when I first heard him speaking at a conference I couldn't believe it, he was a different man.'

'Speaking of new men,' Kate observed, 'they've just appointed the head of the new unit—some American, I think. Apparently they wanted him a few months ago but he wasn't interested, and now, suddenly, he's here. All systems go at last, eh? It'll be lovely not to have to send out burns and plastics off to Bart's, won't it?'

Fliss pushed her plate away, immediately alert. 'What's his name? And how's he going to recruit his team?' She had been waiting for news of this appointment for nearly two months now, ever since the Seymour bequest had been confirmed and the foundations of the new burns and plastic surgery unit that could change her future had been laid.

'It's only just been announced,' Kate said mildly. 'You'll have to do your own detective work if you want to know more. I take it from this reaction that you're still set on getting out of general surgery?'

'You bet!' Fliss said it with rather more feeling than

she'd thought herself capable of mustering in view of her drained state. 'General surgery is fine at the moment, but no one's going to revolutionise appendicectomies or find a brilliant new way of dealing with gallstones. And anyway, I want the kind of surgery where real skill counts. I know I do a beautiful job when I close up—'

'All those years of needlework at school,' murmured Kate cynically.

'It's a matter of patience and skill,' Fliss went on. 'Barney has a nose for the kind of things important in general surgery. He can tell, the moment he opens someone up, what's wrong and where. Do you know, he can find the organs quicker than anyone I've ever seen before?' Kate looked bemused. 'It can actually be very difficult to locate someone's appendix or gall bladder. Every patient's different, you know.' Kate went on eating her sponge pudding; she'd heard it all before. 'And what I'm good at is the very careful work, like suturing and dissecting. I'm not joking, Kate. This isn't just a phase because I'm under pressure at the moment. I want to get into plastic surgery, reconstructive work; one day I want to be a pioneer.'

The other girl laid her hand protectively on top of Fliss's. There was no doubting the sincerity in the junior surgeon's eyes as she spoke about her plans for the future. Felicity Meredith was not, Kate knew, to be trifled with. Under her quiet, unassuming exterior there was a thin layer of sprung steel, a certainty, perhaps even a naïvety, about her hopes and her place in the world. Briefly Kate wondered how much Fliss really knew about the real world. There was something untouched about her; it was as if she had come a long way in a very short time and hadn't stopped to admire the view on the journey. Or perhaps, Kate thought a touch sheepishly, that was her own brand of abrasive wisdom.

'You've got a lot of your father in you, you know,' was all she said.

Fliss's dark eyes didn't flicker in her impassive face. *That* was something she had suspected for a long time—and something she wasn't entirely happy about. 'Enough of this, anyway,' she shrugged lightly. 'Even if I don't wangle my way on to the team, at least we'll have the facilities for burns and so on here. Just think—no more packing people off to all the big hospitals!'

Kate nodded. She was specialising in paediatrics and a surprising number of children came in with burns or facial abnormalities. It was always irksome to have to second them to another hospital, simply for lack of facilities. Apart from the occasional hare lip or skin graft, usually dealt with while patients were also having a more major operation, such cases were rarely seen on Highstead's wards; a pity, for both nursing and medical staff could have done with the experience. But the Seymour bequest was going to put an end to all that.

'Just think of all the technology . . .' mused Kate, her almost black bobbed hair swinging against her cheek as she undid the silver paper round a chocolate bar. 'One of the housemen I talked to about it said that this would be the third biggest unit in the country, and the newest. You'll probably have to do something drastic to get involved.' She paused. 'I wonder what this new chap'll be like?'

'In case I'm called on to sacrifice my body on the examination couch?' Fliss grinned self-deprecatingly. 'I hardly think *that* would influence him!'

'Under that "butter wouldn't melt" look I expect there beats a human heart,' Kate assessed her coolly.

'But you don't do much for the feminine cause by dressing like a man, Fliss. If it wasn't for the skirt you might be a much younger, thinner version of the almighty Morton and his clones. For goodness' sake, it's July outside, and here you are in your best Jaeger suit and blouse, as if it's winter!'

'We surgeons have standards to maintain, and don't forget it!' Fliss cast a slighting glance over her companion's serviceable Madras checked dress, rather creased under the white coat. 'And I don't have one of those,' she flicked the lapel, 'to disguise the fact that I haven't had time to do the ironing!' Her mouth crinkled, betraying her amusement, and Kate laughed, despite the slight stricture.

'I've got to go . . .' They both said it simultaneously and stood up as if on cue. Kate went to bundle up her chocolate wrapper and throw it away, then paused to read it.

'Here,' she said, thrusting it into Fliss's pocket as they made their way out into the public corridors again. 'There's a competition on this—why not do it and win yourself a car?'

'Me and a million others!' If there had been a waste paper basket around Fliss would have thrown the scrap away—but there wasn't, so it stayed in her pocket.

It was the quiet time of the afternoon. Visitors would be allowed in at four; lunches had been finished by one. Medication had been given out, beds made, bodies washed, dressings changed. The nurses were relaxing behind the scenes or doing the quiet sort of tasks that allowed everyone to recoup their strength.

Fliss consciously dulled the click of her smart but practical leather pumps as she strode down the corridors to Women's Medical. Here and there a window let in shafts of sunlight which illuminated the cool passages and hinted at the heat outside in the real world. The smell of cabbage and disinfectant mingled with the aroma of floor polish to create a unique atmosphere; one which Fliss had been exposed to for so many years now, first as a visitor with her father, then as an auxiliary in her year off between school and college and finally as a doctor, that she barely noticed it. Somewhere up ahead of her she could hear the metallic rumble of a trolley making its way to a ward. Funny how, though one could always hear a trolley, even in the middle of the night, one never seemed to meet it, she thought, turning right for Women's Medical. There it was again; the squeak of a protesting wheel, the thrum as it jolted over joins in the lino—but no trolley ever hove into view.

She pushed through the swing doors of Women's Medical and was struck by the faint aroma of flowers, of summer roses cut from someone's garden. A brief thought of her mother rose unbidden to mind; she ought to go and visit soon; then Sister Slater, calm and serene as always, appeared to greet her.

'Good afternoon, Miss Meredith,' she smiled, despite her usual formality. 'I imagine you'd like a cup of tea when you've finished the round—you must be exhausted.'

'That would be lovely,' Fliss agreed, wondering for the dozenth time how Louise Slater could be so thoughtful when she must have had a hard morning of it herself—operating days found other wards in efficient uproar, but Women's Medical always ran like clockwork. She waited while Sister located all the files they would need for the round and arranged for tea to be ready in twenty minutes, then they went together to see

Mrs Morrissey. No comment from Sister Slater about the absence of Barney; not the slightest indication that she in any way mistrusted such a young and *female* surgeon, unlike some of the older Sisters, who implied by looks and offhand comments that a visit from Miss Meredith was second-best.

They stopped at Mrs Morrissey's bedside. She was dozing, looking very pale, the end of her naso-gastric tube taped to her cheek and a saline drip attached to her left arm.

'She came round for a while at eleven-twenty,' Sister consulted her notes. 'She's weak, and this complication will put her back a bit, but thanks to your good timing I'm quite happy with her.'

Fliss ignored the comment. Sister Slater did not give gratuitous compliments, she just said what she thought. 'Good.' Fliss picked up the chart at the end of the bed. 'Her blood pressure is much better. I'll write her up for fifty milligrams of pethidine—she'll be very uncomfortable as soon as she comes round properly, so contact me if you need anything more. And I think we'll have a glucose drip, five per cent, please. She'll need every boost we can give her.'

Sister nodded in agreement and made a note, her neat hands recording the instructions in clear italics. 'She's due for her first aspiration in about an hour,' she said in her calmly modulated voice which gave confidence to surgeon and patient alike.' Shall I arrange for you to see the results immediately?'

'Call me and I'll come over,' Fliss declared. 'And let's have a blood sample down to Path for an iron count as soon as possible, please. I want to be perfectly sure that there's no more haematemesis.'

Bearing in mind that Miss Pope had been comatose on

the operating table four hours ago, she was surprisingly alert—and already complaining of discomfort, her first pain-killing injection, administered in the theatre's recovery room, having begun to wear off.

'I'm afraid you *will* be a little sore,' soothed Fliss, looking through Miss Pope's familiar chart, which she had checked before she came into theatre this morning. 'But everything went according to plan; we repaired your hernia, so you'll soon be feeling the benefit. I'll prescribe something to ease the discomfort now, though.'

'And we'll get you working on those breathing exercises that the physiotherapists taught you the other day,' Sister Slater added firmly. 'It's always better to be able to control the pain yourself rather than have to rely on drugs constantly.'

Miss Pope looked unconvinced, and Fliss and the senior nurse raised knowing eyebrows at each other. It was hospital policy to teach patients as much as possible about pain and posture and muscle control so that they had an alternative to drugs. But some, like Miss Pope, who was middle-aged and overweight, were unwilling to trust anything but a needle.

'Where's the nice young man who came to see me the other day?' she asked suddenly. 'The surgeon.'

'Ah, I think you mean Dr Locke, the anaesthetist,' Fliss replied absentmindedly, signing the drugs authorisation on Miss Pope's chart. '*I'm* the surgeon.'

'*Oh!* You mean that you . . . ?' The thought that Fliss, so open-faced and young-looking, despite her severely tailored suit and authoritative manner, might have wielded the scalpel herself had obviously never crossed Miss Pope's mind. 'I thought it was that older man. It says *Mr Morton* on my bed.' She pointed to the cardboard sign at the head of her bed, where Barney's name was spelt out in large red letters.

'Yes, I'm on Mr Morton's firm,' Fliss assured the patient confidently. 'Don't worry, he was there too—and look how well you're doing! Mrs Hudd over there,' she indicated a bed on the other side of the ward, 'had the same operation as you this morning, with a different firm, and *she's* still half asleep.'

Miss Pope looked slightly placated. 'Oh well,' she sighed, 'I suppose you must know what you're doing . . .'

At her side, Fliss heard Louise Slater swallow a giggle. They completed one more examination, then went back to the Sister's office, where Fliss busied herself for a few minutes, writing up notes and filling in blood test forms. Sister Slater returned with a tray of tea.

Her blue eyes twinkled as she said casually, 'I do hope you know what you're doing, Miss Meredith?'

Fliss chuckled. 'Grrr—they submit themselves to all manner of indignities by teenage medical students, and then they get all miffed because *I've* performed some simple operation!'

'Don't worry, you're beginning to get through. Mrs Rimmer wanted to know why she didn't get visits from the "nice young lady" the other day, and a couple of them have been comparing scars. You'll be in great demand before long for anything above the bikini line!'

Fliss sipped her tea and studied Louise Slater. She was something of a mystery to the whole hospital—serenely attractive, with her ash-blonde hair caught neatly in a French pleat, a tidy figure wearing her uniform with great style. But there was something self-contained about her, distant, as if she didn't want anyone to get too close. And she was renowned as a bit of a tartar on the wards—not the old-fashioned, bossy sort, just a stickler for detail. It didn't help people to sympathise with her that she was naturally so neat and quietly efficient herself; almost superhuman, Fliss had heard disgruntled nurses complain. About her private life there was never a word—no one would dare besmirch such an example of perfect Sisterhood with gossip; no one would dare!

'I would like you to keep an eye on Mrs Wilmott,' Fliss pondered. 'She's too likely a candidate for thrombosis to ignore. She seems to be clotting well enough, but if necessary she'll have to have some more heparin.' Fliss tried not to let her indecision show. The problem was, in such cases, that not even years of experience were enough to predict whether a patient's blood would coagulate and cause a clot. To thin it, heparin was administered: but that might, in turn, stop the operation wound from healing . . .

'I've already asked someone to special her,' Sister Slater commented gently. 'I'll let you know if there's the slightest change in her condition. You know,' she said almost shyly, 'you can't worry about all of them all of the time. We're here to take some of the responsibility too!'

'And thank goodness you are.' Fliss finished her tea, smoothed her navy skirt over her slim thighs and, abashed, made her goodbyes. Men's Medical now—and Sister Walsh . . .

But Sister Walsh was closeted in her room with a patient's relatives. 'Bad news, I'm afraid,' Mandy Price, the senior staff nurse, wrinkled her nose. 'She'll be some time. If you don't mind, I'll do the round with you, Miss Meredith.'

Of course Fliss didn't mind—but she didn't show her

relief. It wasn't good for a surgeon to admit that a member of the nursing staff could strike such terror into her heart. But Sister Walsh's snide distrust and her downright grudging manner when it came to even minor changes in the care of her patients made Fliss both angry and a little nervous. If something were ever to go wrong, she knew that Sister Walsh would be the first to cast aspersions on her competence. Why they had hit it off so badly, Fliss didn't know; she had quietly just put it down to the fact that the middle-aged Sister wasn't very good at taking orders, however carefully couched, from another woman. Particularly from another woman whose record was almost too good to be true and who had settled to an easy, confident relationship with the senior surgeons—a relationship that the other woman envied, having never been able to attain it herself.

Mandy Price was efficient and helpful and didn't raise so much as an eyebrow when Fliss requested that the end of Mr Cawood's bed be raised and that it was time Mr Muller was got out of bed. How much did the staff nurse suffer from Hilda Walsh's sharp tongue and resentful attitude? Fliss found herself worrying. Damn it, it didn't do anyone on the ward any good at all!

'I'll just pop in and see Alfred Emerson on my way out,' she told Nurse Price. 'There's no need to come with me, I just want a chat.' Already the visitors were beginning to arrive and, after the post-prandial nap, cries for bedpans were making themselves heard. Her time as an auxiliary at her local cottage hospital in Oxfordshire had taught Fliss only too well that doctors and surgeons could be remarkably insensitive about the times they chose to call, and she had no desire to make herself unpopular with the nursing staff. Mandy thanked her, took back the notes that she had signed, and said warningly, 'He's getting a bit cantankerous, so watch yourself! He caught Lucy Bingley off guard this morning and pinched her bottom, so he must be getting better.'

'Just let him try it on me!' Fliss drew herself up to her full five feet eight and pulled her sternest face. 'I'll threaten him with another graft if he doesn't behave himself—that should keep you safe for a while!'

Alfred Emerson was in his sixties, a bit of a lad, despite his advancing years. He had been brought in after a night on the tiles had ended with a trial of strength with a bus; the bus had won, unfortunately, and done him a fair bit of damage. And, to speed up the healing of the massive grazing he had received to his lower back and thighs, George Amery, the one surgeon in the hospital qualified to any extent for burns and skin surgery, had made some grafts. Fliss had been on stand-by when Alfred had been brought in, and though he technically wasn't her patient, she often went in to visit him. He didn't have much family, only a rather resigned-looking wife and a grown-up son who was, in response to his father's habits, rather prim and proper and who despaired of Alfred ever accepting his responsibilities.

The son was there now, sitting morosely with his father, as Fliss marched in.

'Hallo, Mr Emerson—Alfred,' she said brightly, aware of the tension in the room. 'How are you today, Alfred? I see they've turned you over again. And Nurse Price tells me you've been enjoying yourself with Nurse Bingley!'

'Dad! What have you been up to this time?' Emerson junior looked scandalised. 'Has he been making a nuisance of himself, Doctor? You know you can't trust him an inch. Even lying here on his stomach he can't be relied upon to behave himself.' He pulled a tight face.

'And there's my mother at home, worried sick and trying
to cope . . . God knows, he isn't much help at the best of
times . . .'

Behind his son's back, Alfred Emerson was pulling
faces and miming to the whining words with such accu-
rate mimicry that Fliss was hard put to it not to laugh.
Oh, Emerson senior was a fool to have got himself in this
fix in the first place, there was no doubt about that. But
he'd borne considerable pain and inconvenience with
stoic acceptance that, having brought it on himself,
it was up to him not to make too much fuss. And he
was a goodhumoured man; once he was well enough
to go back to the ward proper, he'd be a tonic for the
depressed patients.

'If your mother is worried, Mr Emerson,' she interrupted briskly, 'she can talk to a social worker and we'll
try to get something sorted out. As for your father—
well, I think he's learned his lesson now, haven't you,
Alfred?'

'Oh yes, Doctor, I'll never do it again,' responded the
patient with too much eagerness to be sincere. 'I've
learned my lesson. From now on I'll be the most re-
sponsible man you've ever met. Not a drop of alcohol
will touch my lips as long as I shall live . . .' He wiggled
his ears. 'And if you believe that, Doctor, you'll believe
anything,' he chortled.

His son went pink with rage. 'You can see what it's
like with the old fool! How many other people's fathers
go battling with buses? Does yours, Doctor?'

Fliss ignored the idea and opened the door for the son
to leave. 'I'd just like to take a look at your father's graft
sites,' she announced brusquely. 'If you'd just step
outside for a few minutes.'

'And don't come back,' came the response from the

bed. Chastened, the young man left. 'Ah, he's not a bad lad,' Alfred explained as Fliss gently drew back the cover and lifted off the cage that protected the wounds. 'He's just at the stage where he's taking everything seriously—he's engaged and saving to get married and he's worrying about everything; a house, a mortgage, a decent job . . . He hasn't got the time to go worrying about me on top of it all.'

'I see.' Fliss gently lifted off the Melolin dressings that allowed the skin to breathe and yet absorbed any discharge. It was still a mess underneath, but the grafts had taken and slowly replacement skin was beginning to cover what had once been a huge, raw area. Alfred must have been dragged very heavily along the ground for some yards, she reckoned. His shattered right leg had been pieced together by the orthopods and was immobilised in plaster.

'How does it feel?' She kept well away from the exposed area, didn't touch it. Infection of any sort at this stage would be an insurmountable problem.

'Sore. I can't move much at all,' came the heartfelt reply. 'They send round a woman to do exercises on me, but what with me leg and me back . . . It's not much use, Doctor.'

'I know it's difficult, but we've got to keep as much muscle-tone and movement as possible,' Fliss sympathised. 'Keep at it, Mr Emerson.'

She gently placed the dressings back into position and raised that covering his buttocks.

'Cheeky!' he protested. 'And you have the nerve to lecture me on Nurse Bingley?'

The door opened suddenly and Fliss looked up to find Sister Walsh watching critically, her eyes riveted on Mr Emerson's bottom. And behind her, Fliss was aware of another pair of eyes summing up the scene—a pair of eyes belonging to an unknown man.

'No nurse with you, Miss Meredith? I really can't have you prowling my ward unaccompanied,' Hilda Walsh said with a falsely ingratiating smile. 'And Mr Emerson isn't even your patient.'

'Is something wrong here, Sister?' The man pushed forward into the room, hands casually in the pockets of his expensively cut pale grey suit. He looked Fliss up and down with a withering pair of darkest brown eyes that took in her lack of uniform, her hair scraped youthfully back, the almost sexless figure in its severe two-piece . . . She still had the slightly gauche air of a tall schoolgirl whose uniform didn't automatically give her the authority she imagined it did.

'Miss Meredith shouldn't be in here,' Sister Walsh murmured damningly. 'And we *must* try to avoid infection, you know!' She tutted her way across the room and slammed the dressing back over Mr Emerson's sore points.

'Aah!' came his subdued protest.

'That's quite enough of that, Mr Emerson,' Sister quelled him.

The man watched, almost amused, as Fliss stood reluctantly by and let the nurse replace the bed cage and light cover. 'Am I to believe that this hospital permits anyone to wander round the wards, interfering at will, and without supervision, with any patient who takes their fancy?' He raised a puzzled but also very shrewd eyebrow at Fliss, who had been waiting for Sister to put him in the picture and had decided not to waste time trying to justify herself. It would all come out, and then he would be left with egg on his face; that was enough for her, whoever he was—hospital visitor, new administrator, potential new doctor, whatever. But Sister Walsh found something to tidy on the bedside cabinet and remained stubbornly quiet.

'Well, what have you got to say for yourself?'

A tiny fuse of anger sparked in Fliss's bosom; a flash of Kate's militancy must have sown itself in her during lunch, for she glared at him with out-and-out distaste—and found herself absorbing the impression of Italianate dark looks, an exceptionally long, elegant nose and the kind of thin, well-defined mouth normally seen in the sixteenth-century paintings of southern European aristocrats in the National Gallery—not that she'd had the leisure to go there for some time.

'Before I explain to you the facts of the case, would you be kind enough to inform me of your identity and your interest in this patient?' she asked with frosty politeness. How dared he look at her like this, as if she was some incompetent! Would he speak to a man in this way? Gosh, Fliss reflected, as that thought flashed through her mind, she *had* begun to sound like Kate! And to be honest, yes; this man was the sort of arrogant, contemptuous egomaniac who would talk to *anyone* in this fashion.

'Nicholas Da Costa.' He held out his hand briefly and as she went half-heartedly to shake it, drew it away again, leaving Fliss with her arm in mid-air and a confused look on her face. Sister Walsh tried to keep her smile under wraps. 'I have just been appointed to direct and develop the Seymour Memorial unit. Perhaps you have heard of it,' he said scathingly, but the tightness of his lips indicated that he thought it unlikely. 'And now I would like to know what you are doing here, interfering with my patient.'

'*Your* patient?' Fliss couldn't prevent a note of disbelief entering her voice. 'Well, this is the first I've heard of it!' She drew herself up to her full five feet eight and stood firm on soles that had carried her since the early hours of the morning almost without break. 'I am here because I assisted Mr Amery with Mr Emerson's skin grafts when he was brought in. And,' she turned sharply to Sister,' I told Staff Nurse Price to go back to the ward where she was needed rather than hang around here getting bored with me. I don't know, Mr Emerson, I'm obviously not trusted an inch around here, am I?'

Had she gone too far? she wondered, seeing the fury cross both faces watching her. 'I know the feeling, Doctor,' the patient said wanly.

'Be quiet, Mr Emerson!' Sister silenced him.

'You're a surgeon at this hospital?' Nicholas Da Costa seemed to doubt it.

'Yes, I am. And Sister knows it. Why she didn't feel it necessary to inform you, I can't say. But if Mr Emerson is to be transferred into your hands I'll leave you with him. But never fear, Alfred,' she bent to his side so that he could see her, 'I'll pop in and see you some time.'

With the merest of nods to Sister and trying to ignore the man she had to slip past to escape, Fliss made her exit. Apologising to Mandy Price for the pasting she would probably receive, she dashed to the cloakroom and locked herself in a cubicle before she allowed the true impact of what she had just done and said to hit her.

Her hands were balled in rage, her jaw ached where she had clenched it for so long . . . Fliss knew, with as much certainty as she knew she was damn well in the right, that she had made an enemy. She hadn't merely got off on the wrong foot with a man whom she should have cultivated—oh no, that could be rectified. What she had to accept was that she had utterly destroyed any chance of getting involved in the work of the Seymour unit. For after that scene, that act of spontaneous mutual contempt, she didn't imagine that she'd be able to look him in the eye, again, let alone grovel to him!

CHAPTER TWO

IT was just gone eight o'clock. The sun was falling in the sky and casting a seductive glow over the already attractive streets of Highstead as Fliss walked miserably up the hill towards her home. The trees at the roadside didn't please her, as usual; the roses growing so abundantly in front gardens might just as well have not been there. Oh, this could have been such a good day. Mrs Morrissey had come round and managed to sit up only half an hour ago, and tests had revealed that the haemorrhage had ceased. Mr Cawood's blood pressure had recovered nicely. Miss Pope had decided to stage a competition with Mrs Hudd to see who could get better quicker and had spent the afternoon alternately dozing and doing her breathing exercises, according to an amused Sister Slater. If only Fliss hadn't had a spare few minutes to spend with Mr Emerson, everything would be perfect still . . .

She turned off the main thoroughfare at the antique shop on the corner of her road, passed the pub, where smart wrought iron chairs and tables had been put out for the wine-drinking clientele—no bitter drinkers in Highstead—and approached the house she shared with Peter and Jane, who was a fairly junior executive in a public relations firm. A motley crew, perhaps, but they seemed to get on well enough. Peter had the semi-basement flat and made up in the garden what he lost in terms of a view and light. Fliss had the ground floor and had the minor inconvenience of being aware of the comings and goings of the others. And Jane lived on top and tried to be as quiet as possible for the sake of her dedicated medical friends. Apart from the odd party, or people in the garden when Peter wanted to sleep, it was a civilised way of life.

The garden needed weeding, Fliss thought gloomily as she searched for her front door key in her bag. And if someone didn't prune back that rampant climbing rose this autumn, by next year they wouldn't be able to get in or out of the flats!

'Don't lock the door!' Jane flew up the garden path, her high heels catching dangerously in the rather worn paving, and Fliss held it wide for her. 'Thanks,' she smiled as they stood in the hallway. 'How about coming up and having a drink with me—I've had some good news!'

Fliss shook her head reluctantly. 'You're welcome to come in and have a cup of tea with me,' she offered, 'but then I'm having a bath and going straight to bed.'

'If I won't be in the way, I'd love to.'

It was stiflingly warm and they both went immediately to open the windows. The sound of Peter playing his flute wafted up through the still evening air, and Fliss's heart felt lighter.

'Shall I go down and invite him?' questioned Jane, knowing that Fliss and Peter were old friends, though she wasn't really sure quite how things were between them. Fliss couldn't have put her straight; she herself wasn't sure quite where she stood in Peter's volatile affections, either.

'No. If he's playing I never bother him,' she said simply, darting into her tiny kitchen to put the kettle on.

'I *do* like your place, Fliss.' Jane walked round the sitting-room, picking things up and putting them down, seemingly oblivious to the piles of books and magazines,

the flattened cushions on the old chintz sofa that
was beginning to go at the seams a bit, the chipped
Staffordshire figures on the mantelpiece which Fliss had
collected years ago, as a child, before they became too
expensive for her to contemplate.

'I'd like it too, if it wasn't so dusty. At least all your
high-tec stuff is easy to clean and dirty marks don't show
on black leather . . .' Selfconscious, Fliss noticed
another smudge on the well-washed loose covers of her
squashy armchair. She moved over to remove the three
empty mugs and plates from the ring-marked coffee
table—evidence of her last three meals, coffee and
Marmite on toast, each one.

'Look, let me give you a hand . . .' offered Jane,
discovering another one hidden behind a lush fern that
grew up one side of the pretty Victorian cast-iron fireplace.

'I'd rather you didn't,' Fliss said bashfully, loath to
permit access to the white and yellow kitchen where her
washing was soaking in the sink and assorted pots and
pans awaited the washing-up bowl. She hated to be
caught out like this; though she had never been a
fastidiously neat person she didn't want Jane to get the
idea that she always lived like this. But for the past five
days she had scarcely had ten minutes to do things like
cleaning and Hoovering.

It didn't take long for the kettle to boil, and then they
sat on the sofa and Jane told fiendishly funny stories
about the internal politics of her office; all about how
Carol had been demoted because she went off for a
weekend with Ted and how Jane had triumphed by
winning a contract to promote a major new perfume.
'Here,' she said, riffling through her executive-style
briefcase, 'have a free sample,' and she handed Fliss a

large bottle of expensive-looking liquid. 'You look as if you needed cheering up,' she insisted when Fliss protested that she couldn't possibly accept it. 'And free gifts are all part of the perks of the job. If you can't use it now, put it away and bring it out when you want to impress someone.'

'Thanks—I do need cheering up,' Fliss agreed. 'I've just blown the next step in my career ladder.' It was all right to talk to Jane like that. She had her career in PR planned almost to the month, including promotions and pay-rises. If the agency didn't come up trumps, she just reorganised her schedule and left, declaring that they didn't know what they'd lost. And at twenty-three, though still relatively junior, she was already earning enough to start thinking about a mortgage and a flat of her own.

'Oh no!' she wailed sympathetically as all the dreadful details were recounted—from Alfred's patchwork bottom to the moment when Fliss had turned on her heel and walked out on them all. 'He doesn't know your name,' was all the comfort she could offer as Fliss grimly refilled their cups.

'Oh, Sister will have told him,' Fliss sighed. 'It wasn't so much that I was rude; but I made a fool of him in front of a Ward Sister and a patient, though it was all Sister Walsh's fault, really. She set me up in a way.'

'I expect he'll appreciate that. And if he was so nasty to a complete stranger think how awful he might be to the people working with him. He sounds a right toad! I think you're best out of it, Fliss, I really do. Just think, you might have been lured on to his team, only to discover too late that he's the most objectionable man in the world!'

'All I want is the opportunity,' muttered Fliss quietly,

as much to herself as Jane. She took the pins out of her hair and let it fall in its uncompromisingly straight fashion, bobbed, to her shoulders. It was strange how readily a picture of him came back to her—how vividly she could see his features in her mind's eye, how clearly hear the quiet contempt in his voice.

Fliss woke in panic from a deep sleep and found herself grappling with the sheet that was all the covering on her bed during the present hot spell. In the sitting-room the telephone was shrilling. When she finally managed to escape the grasp of the sheet, still sleep-filled, she reached for her alarm clock. Five-thirty. What on earth could they want her for at five-thirty?

'Sorry to disturb you . . .' Andy Lee, the duty officer, sounded about as apologetic as if he had interrupted her lunch break. 'We've got a surgical case here—nothing major; someone out jogging on the Heath managed to impale one of his legs on a bit of railing . . .'

Fliss knew too well not to ask questions like *how*, and *why* and what was anyone doing out at this time of the morning, but merely stated that she'd be there in ten minutes and put the phone down before calling the local taxi firm and arranging for a driver to call immediately. Shrugging out of her extra-large T-shirt, which she favoured for night wear, she threw on a sweater and jeans and remembered to take with her her newly cleaned cream suit and some tights; only God knew when she'd see the flat again. With the bed unmade, the washing still hanging over the bath to dry and the draining board stacked high with mugs and plates, she fled.

Highstead didn't have a full-scale A and E department; there were too many large central London hospi-

tals with extensive casualty units within only ten minutes'
ambulance journey to justify a full complement of
casualty officers and staff. But they did provide limited
cover for purely local incidents, most of which came in
during the day and could be dealt with by the outpatients
and minor surgery departments. It was rare, though, for
there to be a surgical emergency. Fliss wondered how
bad it might be and hoped, at the back of her mind, that
she wouldn't be called upon to do anything too ambitious. She still didn't feel fully alert.

The sun was up already and beginning to warm the air.
Hair down, feet in flat sandals, a very different Felicity
Meredith from the one who had left the night before
entered the Victorian portals of the hospital, savoured
for another day the *eau de Dettol* and the distant squeak
of a phantom trolley.

'Ah, here you are,' Andy Lee gestured her towards a
cubicle in the makeshift casualty area. 'Come and see
what you think.'

A young man, pale and clammy, was stretched out on
trolley. He was dressed in running gear, tiny white shorts
showing off long, muscular legs and a brief singlet
finishing crucially above his flat brown abdomen.

The latest form of exhibitionism, Fliss thought dryly
to herself before getting down to the matter in hand. For
in addition to his required dress he was also attached to a
piece of familiar black iron railing—a spike, about nine
inches long, had pierced his leg just above his ankle.

'Oh dear,' she murmured sympathetically. 'Do we
have any X-rays, Dr Lee?' If he had shattered a bone or
a ligament then he would really need the attentions of a
specialist.

'Yes, here.' The duty officer held the plates up to the
light box, out of view of the patient, for Fliss to see. 'In

fact, it couldn't have done less damage, as you can see. It's really just a matter of removing it, Miss Meredith.'

Fliss ran a practised eye over the picture. Apparently the spike has missed his Achilles tendon and passed cleanly between his tibia and fibula. The only real danger was a haemorrhage when the missile was removed, and forewarned was forearmed in surgical practice.

'Well, Mr . . . Lyon,' she consulted his notes, 'things don't look nearly as bad as they must seem to you at the moment. Can I just ask you to tell me what happened?'

The man grimaced and looked dubiously at Fliss's scrubbed face. Male doctors, called out on duty without notice, had the benefit of a beard to make them look rakishly masculine; Fliss's face merely looked pale and even younger than usual. 'I was out jogging,' he began. 'I have to go out early because I'm a solicitor and I don't have any time during the day. I normally get on to the Heath down by the ponds; the railings there have fallen over at an angle. I usually jump over them, but this morning I lost my footing and fell back on them . . .' He trailed off, still slightly shocked.

'How was he brought in?' Fliss asked the duty officer.

'Fire Brigade—they had to cut him out,' said Andy.

'Are you in pain?' Fliss turned back to the patient and gently manipulated his foot. Despite the nightmarish look of the injury, Mr Lyon didn't wince.

'That's the funny part,' he admitted. 'It hurt like hell when I first did it, but now it's just a dull throb.'

Fliss nodded and ran the end of her Biro down the centre of the sole of his foot. His reflex was fine—his toes curled immediately. Motioning to the nurse to lift the patient's singlet, she listened to his chest, looked at his blood pressure readings. Everything seemed right.

'What we'll do is remove it under a local anaesthetic, Mr Lyon,' she decided. 'That way you'll be up and out of here all the quicker. I'll arrange for you to have an injection to relax you now and I'll see you in theatre in about half an hour.'

'How long is all this going to take?' he asked fractiously. 'I'm supposed to be in court at ten.'

'I doubt whether you'll get to court today,' Fliss replied calmly. 'But if all goes well, and there's no reason why it shouldn't, you'll be there tomorrow. If you give Nurse any messages she'll pass them on.' The man sighed exaggeratedly and lay back, resigned.

'I'll write him up for a low dose of omnopon now,' Fliss told Andy Lee. 'It'll keep him quiet and that leg relaxed. It's nearly six-fifteen,' she consulted her watch. 'Would you call out the duty anaesthetist and a theatre nurse?'

'Sister McIlvaney will be in soon,' Andy reminded her. 'She's got Mr Amery's list this morning and she's always in extra early for him.'

'Fine.' Fliss couldn't fault Sister's experience, even if she was rather a tartar. 'Get Mr Lyon cross-matched, just in case.'

As it turned out, there was no need to have worried about cross-matching Mr Lyon's blood. He lay, slightly sedated but still awake, in theatre number two while Fliss used all her strength to remove the spike from his leg and eventually had to request the help of Sister. Many jokes had been made about Sister's bulk and physique, which qualified her for throwing the shot for some obscure East European country, but today Fliss welcomed her strong wrist.

'Oooh!' The patient sighed in relief as the pressure in

his leg was released. Scrupulously avoiding direct contact with the spike, which had been sterilised as far as possible before the patient was admitted to theatre, Fliss laid it into a kidney dish and proceeded to irrigate the wound. There wasn't much blood loss at all.

'It's amazing, isn't it?' Peter Locke echoed her thoughts as Fliss marvelled at how lightly Mr Lyon had escaped more serious injury. Peter had arrived in a good mood, had administered the lignocaine to the patient's leg and was now watching the clock, calculating if, and when, more of the local anaesthetic would be required.

Deftly Fliss injected antibiotic into the wound. Then she packed it lightly, having inserted four sutures, and Mr Lyon was wheeled from the theatre.

'Thank you very much for coming in,' she acknowledged Sister and Peter.

'I would have been in anyway,' Sister dismissed the courtesy in her usual uncompromising style.

'Have some breakfast and clean up, and then we can go the rounds of yesterday's patients together,' Peter suggested. As anaesthetist he had to check his patients for the twenty-four hours after their operations. This morning would be his final call on Mrs Morrissey and Co.

Fliss held out the kidney dish containing the spike. 'Here, clean this up and then give it to Mr Lyon. Think how impressive it'll be for him to produce it and tell everyone he had it stuck in his leg!'

With a chuckle, Peter took the bit of iron and disappeared back to his prep room.

Knowing that today she wasn't due for theatres, Fliss took a quick shower with the toiletries she kept in her locker, made up her face lightly to meet the public, and stepped into her coffee and cream striped shirt-dress, over which she wore a light cream linen jacket with shoulder pads. Her hair, freshly washed after last night, she left down in its softening bob. She thought, looking in the tiny mirror on the changing room wall—for after all, this was really a male domain, and men didn't need things like full-length mirrors—that she looked almost ridiculously smart for seven-thirty in the morning.

On her way back through the surgeons' sitting-room, she glanced over the notice board, just to check any changes to routine. Had anyone suggested that she was looking for some news of the awful Mr Da Costa, Fliss would have denied it vehemently. But her eye fell with unerring accuracy on the hastily typed note that announced that a reception party to welcome him was to be held this evening in the senior staff common room and that all surgical staff were hereby invited. Well, *I'm not going*, she thought instantly—only to be surprised by a twinge of disappointment which caught her quite unawares. Damn it, anyone would think she wanted to see him again, she thought, confused, when in fact the truth of the matter was that she could happily go through life without hearing his name mentioned again.

But she didn't have the luck to avoid him as she crossed the reception area on her way to the canteen five minutes later, for Nicholas Da Costa was, even at this early hour of the morning, supervising the erection of a series of display stands on which he was arranging the architect's plans for the Seymour unit and a variety of informative pictures and articles about Highstead Hospital and the modern treatment of burns and physical abnormalities. Already, half finished, it looked impressive. Fliss tried to ignore the desire to go up and take a further look, tried to stride nonchalantly on her way. But Mr Da Costa was having none of that.

'What do you think, Miss Meredith?' he asked pointedly, refusing to allow Fliss to sneak past.

She stood and pondered for a moment, determined not to blush and falter. Nick Da Costa stood, hands on hips, the top button of his Oxford cloth shirt, with its buttoned-down collar, loose, his slim blue tie dangling casually. Fliss stared desperately at a before and after picture of a talipes calcaneus, aware only of the fact that, though she should dislike the man thoroughly, the only thing to fill her mind at the moment was irrational interest in the dark hair that was peeping from beneath his shirt at the neck. She had never before felt this way about anyone; why had her professional equilibrium deserted her now?

Nick studied her while she studied the pictures. Her eyes seem to have fixed on a rather gruesome photo of a child with a deformed face. He had wondered whether it was a bit strong himself, before he had selected it from his private collection of information to be put on display. How cool and collected she was! He wondered what she was doing here at this time of the morning, looking as if she was due to go to Ascot . . .

What on earth can I say? Fliss panicked, aware of his eyes on her and knowing that whatever she said was bound to be wrong. But she'd be damned if she was going to be too sice to him!

How cool can you get? Nick wondered as she took a long, slow survey of the display. But that wasn't surprising—she was Mortimer Meredith's daughter, wasn't she? Cool and calculating as ice; as hard-headed as her father. No wonder she'd got so far so quickly. He had asked around after yesterday's fiasco to find out more about her; she wasn't more than twenty-six, and from what he could hear, she was holding Barney Morton's firm together. Well, she didn't need anything to boost her confidence, evidently—which was lucky, because he wasn't going to give her an inch.

'Some people might be a bit worried by this,' she gestured to the picture of the child and he swore silently. Trust her, trust Mortimer's daughter, to have the same instinct for demolishing people as her father! She turned to face him; he took in the careful make-up, the flawless skin, the soft hair, and he didn't register the rather plain features, the fact that the hair was an undistinguished brown. Instead he felt a quiet ire that she should be standing here so bandbox smart while he, who had been up all night, hadn't managed to shave or tame his unruly hair. And he felt a flicker of something else, too, which he instantly blocked from his mind.

'I don't happen to believe that people should be coddled and protected from the nasty things of this world,' he responded gruffly, trying to roll down his sleeves as he spoke. 'And Cruzon's Disease treatment has been one of the major breakthroughs of the past few years.'

'Oh, I know—I've been following the developments,' Fliss chipped in.

How smug, Nick Da Costa thought; oh, sugar, thought Fliss—now I've blown it completely!

She stared down at his wrist, noting the discreet gold watch that circled his powerful but lean arm; the dark hair, the long fingers. Panic and simultaneous excitement swept through her in a wave that she couldn't have stopped, or explained, if she'd tried.

'Well,' she smiled with an effort, 'I suppose I'd better go and get some breakfast.' She hesitated a moment longer, almost as if she wanted to prolong the agony for him. 'Do you intend working on Cruzon cases in the

Seymour unit?' It was a highly dangerous and specialised area of surgery, involving, as it did, the eye sockets and the cranium. It was just the kind of surgery that Fliss had longed for—and doubted that she would ever get the chance to experience.

'Eventually,' Nick Da Costa said stiffly, and turned back to what he had been doing when she had tripped through reception. Why was she so interested anyway? A thought occurred to him, a thought so disturbing that he jabbed himself with a drawing pin. Surely she wasn't angling for a place on the new Seymour team? No. He would never have Sir Mortimer Meredith's daughter working for *him*!

The morning flew past in the state of organised chaos that all outpatient clinics descend to; people were early or late. Barney and Fliss did what they could to keep to schedule, but soon the half-dozen patients waiting outside the consulting room swelled to a dozen or more. They worked without a break, trying to sort those who urgently needed treatment from those who were simply mildly uncomfortable and fit them all into some sort of order.

'We can take Blanchard in next week, if there's a bed for him,' muttered Fliss, running her pencil up and down the operating lists. 'And Mrs Raitz opted for private treatment, so if you want to fit Lessiter into her slot we can manage.'

The fact that their stomachs were rumbling hurried them through the files. One patient referred to the radiography department here; an appointment made with another specialist there. Routine cases added to the lists; the occasional patient referred back to the GP. While Fliss updated the files and paperwork, Barney went next door to the firm's secretary, Sue Pickton, and dictated letters and arranged for appointments.

Fliss finished her part of the job at gone two and staggered into the staff canteen for a late lunch. And then, with Barney away giving a lecture to a group of nursing students seconded from St Margaret's—for Highstead didn't have a school of nursing of its own—she began the afternoon's work. Consent forms for operations and routine post-operative checks for those who needed them—it never seemed to stop.

It was Sister Walsh's afternoon off on Men's Surgical, so Fliss breezed in and was met by a chastened Mandy Price. 'I think you might have a bit of a problem with bed three,' said Mandy. 'Mr Locke's there with him.'

Fliss made her way to the cubicle with the flowered orange curtains round it, and once again thought that whoever had chosen them back in the sixties, when flower-power and fluorescence had been all the rage, ought to have to live with them at home now. She checked her notes before she entered the sanctum. Mr Rose, aged sixty-one, hernia, admitted today for surgery tomorrow. Everything seemed straightforward—she wondered what the problem could be.

'Ah, Miss Meredith!' Peter straightened up from where he had been examining Mr Rose's chest, and the gentleman hurriedly pulled his pyjama jacket across his chest and blushed an impressive crimson.

'Dr Locke, Mr Rose . . .' Fliss nodded to each, maintaining her professional poise.

'It's the Reverend Mr Rose, actually,' Peter smiled. 'I've just been explaining that you won't actually be doing the operation, *Miss Meredith*.' His eyebrows were shooting up and down as he spoke, and Fliss wondered curiously what was going on.

'Oh, but I will,' she inserted, coming over to shake the gentleman's hand. He gave her a clammy paw and then withdrew nervously under the blanket, clearing his throat. Peter stood at the end of the bed and looked irritated.

'I don't think I can consent to that,' said Mr Rose at last in a nervous voice. 'As Dr Locke has pointed out, I'm a man of the cloth . . . I really don't think . . .'

There was an awkward silence as Fliss digested this. She had met some embarrassed patients before, but this took the cake. Gently she sat down by the bed. 'I *am* fully qualified, you know. And I won't actually be in charge of the operation. It will be performed by Mr Morton, whom you saw last month.'

The man looked relieved, and Fliss crossed her fingers and hoped that she'd told the truth. If Barney was feeling lazy or pushed for time, she might be the one to fix this patient's hernia. She had hoped to examine Mr Rose now, too, but that was obviously out of the question.

'Mr Morton didn't tell me he had a female assistant,' he ventured, almost aggrieved, as if some awful plot had been sprung on him.

'Women get everywhere these days, don't they?' Peter defused the situation from his station by the end of the bed. And then, remembering that the Church was still an all-male bastion, he became embarrassed too.

'I shall send Mr Morton to see you this evening, Mr Rose,' Fliss decided to give in gracefully. She left the cubicle and found Mandy Price waiting outside. They walked solemn-faced to the office and only allowed themselves a wide smile when the door was safely shut.

'He won't allow a female nurse near him,' Mandy

protested, 'and we've only got one male nurse! What'll we do when he has to have a catheter or a bath?'

'I'm going to leave that to Sister Walsh,' Fliss declared stoutly, with only the slightest hint of malice. 'I suggest you let *her* worry about it, Mandy.'

'I did try to warn you!' Peter was telling the story to a small group of senior staff congregated in one corner of the common room. Fliss had missed the speeches and the formal introduction of Nicholas Da Costa; was too late for his amusing address and only just in time to recognise the admiring looks he was drawing from the few senior female staff who had come along. Mrs Wilmott, who had promised to be a problem all along, had chosen just that time to develop a thrombosis which, fortunately, had been spotted in good time and was even now being dispersed. Barney and Fliss had spent the last half hour running tests and trying to ease things for her, and Fliss was flustered when she strode at her boss's heels into the gathering.

'Have a glass of wine, my dear,' Sister McIlvaney held one out for her. 'But not too much, mind. You mustn't go enjoying yourself too much!' She laughed heartily, and Fliss giggled from sheer fear. Sister didn't believe in fun; she believed in one glass because research showed that the occasional glass of wine or dram of malt did no harm—in fact might even do some good. But anything more was wicked.

'Poor man!' Fliss wheeled round to Peter again. 'I don't suppose any woman but his mother has ever seen him without his pyjamas on. He's never had anything wrong with him before—it must have been a shock.'

'Has Barney been round?' asked Peter.

'Just now. Mr Rose signed, apparently, with great

reluctance and would like all the ladies present to leave the theatre when the moment comes!'

'There's nothing wrong with modesty,' Sister McIlvaney reminded them sternly. 'In fact, many people would say that it's sadly lacking in today's generation.'

'Yes, Sister,' the small group of youthful doctors chorused repentantly.

'I see now why you're so keen to get into the Seymour team,' said Kate, a playful look in her eye. 'Must admit, I'd try it too if I had a chance.'

Fliss glanced at Peter, wondering whether she would see anything like jealousy in his calmly handsome face. But she didn't. If he had heard, he couldn't care less. Perhaps she should have felt a pang—but she didn't. She had met Peter years ago at medical school. Like hers, his family were all in medicine; like her he had been channelled into it from an early age. Sometimes Fliss wondered whether he regretted it—he certainly went through patches of tremendous discontent with the job. Fliss sympathised with him to a great extent. Vital though the anaesthetist's position was, it didn't carry the glamour that went with the title 'surgeon'. But then, she considered, he had decided fairly early on in his career that he didn't want all the stresses that went with surgical training.

She looked across and found him watching the others chatting, a familiar faraway look on his pleasant, open face, and she suddenly realised how little she really knew about what went on in his head. He was a difficult man to know, with his attacks of moodiness and his exacting standards. He only seemed to let himself go in his music—never with her, and she considered herself his closest friend. They had worked together, spent their off-duty hours together at times, had sometimes kissed and cuddled . . . but she didn't think of him in a sexual way, she realised with a start. He was familiar, safe, distant; all the things that a man like Nick Da Costa wasn't. A flush swept Fliss's face as she acknowledged with silent embarrassment that Peter was the only man she really knew out of work; she had purposely kept away from personal relationships while she was train- ing—not that a great number were offered, for she knew that she had put people off with her dedication and high standards. Peter was a bit like that too, he somehow managed to fend off anything outside his small world . . . In a moment of blinding revelation, Fliss realised what both of them had been doing. They had been hiding behind a non-existent relationship so that they wouldn't have to get involved in the real world of emotional turbulence and pain.

A large paw of a hand grabbed her elbow and she was roused from her reverie, a distant, reflective look on her face as Barney drew Mr Da Costa into the group and introduced them one by one. Now the new unit leader was dressed in a light linen suit, his hair slicked down, his chin recently shaved, almost unrecognisable as the approachable man of this morning.

'And this is Felicity Meredith, my junior registrar,' Barney left her until last and laid something like a proprietorial hand on Fliss's shoulder. Fliss nodded noncommittally and Nicholas Da Costa bestowed an ambiguous half-smile on her. There was silence for a moment and then Kate began to ask questions about the new unit.

'I saw your display in reception,' she smiled engag- ingly. 'It's a very good idea. When do you imagine the unit will be operative?'

Nick Da Costa turned his back gratefully on Fliss. There was something about the girl's even brown stare, the slightest hint of her father's manner, that disconcerted him.

'By the end of October, with any luck,' he responded. 'The basic plans have already been drawn up. I've asked for a few changes, mainly to accommodate the latest technology, but the groundwork has already been completed, which is good news.'

'I suppose you'll be recruiting staff before too long?' Kate asked casually. Fliss froze; she couldn't see her friend's face, but she could hear a mischievous lilt to her voice.

Nick's neck began to prickle, almost as if he could sense the interest of the tall woman standing silent behind him. He raised his glass and took a mouthful of cheap red wine, working out how he could firmly put the ambitious Miss Meredith in her place without appearing rude in front of all these pleasant people.

He shrugged engagingly. 'I don't know the situation as yet,' he admitted with a benign smile, 'but bearing in mind the unit is completely new and that we have to establish its reputation quickly, I will most probably recruit from outside Highstead. We'll need experienced people with a proven track record in the field. Later, in a few years' time, perhaps we can start bringing in raw young recruits to train.' A flicker of disappointment crossed Kate's face and he wondered whether she, too, was on the lookout for a prestigious new position. God preserve him from the women at this hospital! he thought cynically.

'That's a great pity. I'm sure there are plenty of capable staff who'd love the opportunity to develop their expertise—though obviously we wouldn't want to lose too many of them! I know Fliss, for one, was hoping for the opportunity.'

Nick Da Costa and Kate turned to confront Fliss, who was aware of the selfconscious flush of her face and the disappointment lurching in her stomach.

'I'm sorry to disappoint you,' he said without much sincerity, taken aback by the genuine distress on her strong face.

'Oh, don't worry,' she tried bravely, 'I revised my plans not long ago, and working on the Seymour unit is no longer among them.' How would he feel if he knew that this change had happened last night, after meeting him? Kate cast her a disbelieving frown but said nothing.

'You sound very ambitious.' Mr Da Costa's eyebrows rose and the twinkle in his eye suggested that he *did* know. 'It's obviously a streak that runs in the family. Are you intending to follow in your father's footsteps?' He lifted his glass nonchalantly to his lips, as if he didn't realise the bombshell he'd just dropped.

'Oh, no,' Fliss said firmly before she quite realised how disloyal to her father it sounded. How did he know, anyway? She rebelled at the idea of him having the advantage of her. 'Are you acquainted with my father?' she asked, as if she thought it most unlikely.

'Oh yes. In fact I saw Sir Mortimer,' he pronounced the name as if it was something nasty, 'only a month ago, when he dropped out of a project I'd spent nearly a year organising at Princetown medical school.' A bell rang in Fliss's head, something about her father deciding he couldn't tie himself up in research for such a long period. 'We were going to work together on patients who had lost their sight after nerve injuries to the cranium and face; I'd have done the structural side and your father was vital for the eyes. The project folded, of course.'

There was a long silence. Fliss had heard about it in her father's letters but had never realised it had hinged so totally on him. The realisation of just how important and powerful Sir Mortimer was came as a surprise.

Nick watched her earnest face with surprise, too, wondering what it could be about the firm, rather plain features that made him want to get to know the woman behind them. He was attracted to the plain-speaking person, the unaffected character, that he imagined behind them. But then her chin came up confidently and those dark Meredith eyes, so apparently gentle, so deceptive, looked coolly through him.

'Of course,' he shrugged quickly, 'Princetown's loss is Highstead's gain, if that's not too immodest. When I was first invited to lead this team I had to say no. So Sir Mortimer should be given the credit for getting the Seymour off the ground. Now,' he looked at his watch, 'I must go. Thank you all for your friendly welcome. I shall see you all round the hospital, I'm sure.'

With further brief farewells to the other clusters of staff, he zigzagged his way across the room and out into the corridor.

'Oh *dear*!' Kate's sigh said it all. Fliss's mind whirled with conflicting thoughts—of revenge, of anger with her father for being at the root of all this, and with sneaking awareness that she'd been aiming too high anyway.

'Excuse me.' Suddenly, teeth gritted, mind made up, she knew what she had to do to make this whole thing bearable, and she followed that arrogant back out of the room, down the corridor and along to the offices occupied by the heads of surgery and medicine.

Her flying entrance into his office caught Nick off guard. He was just unbuttoning his shirt, ready to change into something less formal for his evening with a willing staff nurse who had all but thrown herself into his arms on the children's ward, when Felicity Meredith, full of icily suppressed fury, burst in on him.

'*Mr* Da Costa . . .' she began, then faltered as she took in his state of undress and his darkly haired chest. His mouth twisted with amused tolerance.

'Yes?' He couldn't help it. She looked so staggered, so charmingly nonplussed that he regretted for a moment that she was the daughter of a man he had sworn he would never have anything to do with again.

'I just came to say that I'm sorry that my father let you down so badly but that I hope you won't hold it against me. We've started off badly and I'd like to think that despite what's happened we can have a properly professional relationship . . .' Unconsciously she wrung her hands and her mouth tightened into an anxious line. At the end of the day, with her make-up gone and her eyes tired, she looked very much more human than she had early that morning.

'Sit down.' He waved to a chair, then sat easily on the desk at her side and did up his buttons again. Fliss watched from under lowered lashes, aware of that strange chemical reaction happening inside her again. 'I've got nothing against you, and I've got to apologise for that misunderstanding yesterday. I'm afraid I got the wrong end of the stick—and you didn't look like a surgeon, you know, Fliss . . .' He tried out her diminutive name and found that it left him needing to swallow. Fliss said nothing. 'You must be good to have come so far in the hospital, and I've heard nothing but good about you.' He deliberately didn't mention Sister Walsh's opinion because he wasn't sure whether hers was a judgment on which he would like to rely, but all the same, he bore it in mind. 'What I mean is that I'm sorry if you felt there were any insinuations about your capacity as a surgeon in what I said—and I'm sure that we can establish a useful professional relationship . . .'

Fliss smiled to herself. It always worked. A little humility, a little kow-towing, and the great men always changed their tunes. She looked up and gave him a knowing smile. 'Good,' was all she said, but the gleam in her eyes told him what had happened.

'You're very young, of course,' he bit back, getting off the desk and standing over her threateningly while he lectured himself for being foolish enough to be taken in by her apparent humility, 'and my kind of work is very stressful, particularly for a woman, so I suggest you consolidate your . . .'

'There we have it, don't we?' Fliss climbed casually to her feet. She was tall and he was taller, but for the moment she didn't notice that. 'I am Sir Mortimer Meredith's daughter and I'm a woman; what more heinous crime could there be? And despite the fact that I'm a good surgeon, as you yourself just admitted, that disqualifies me from being taken seriously . . .' She would have gone on, but there was a knock on the door and a young nurse, bra-less and pertly pretty in a low-cut summer vest and gathered skirt, made her glowing entry. She smiled briefly at Fliss, then glued her eyes to Nick.

'I'll say goodbye.' Fliss looked at them both knowingly, then exited through the haze of perfume that had accompanied the young nurse. She could not imagine how things could possibly be worse; her plans were shattered, her confidence undermined, her calm way of life disturbed. But at least she had the knowledge that Nick Da Costa, despite his too-good-to-be-true looks and reputation, was prejudiced, chauvinistic and a womaniser to boot, and that made her feel slightly less than suicidal.

CHAPTER THREE

It was almost midday when Fliss emerged from the surgeons' changing rooms—where she, as the only woman on the teams, had her own cubicle—having spent the morning working with Mr Deakin, the ortho-paedic specialist. They had sewn two fingers back on the hand of a child who had been bitten by a Jack Russell terrier, and Fliss had been allowed to assist in the delicate nerve and tendon work. She was feeling pleased with herself; she loved anything new, craved knowledge, wanted to feel that she could do almost anything that might be asked of her.

In Barney's office she checked the trays and files that held her own work. There were some pre-operative checks to be done and half a dozen patients to see, but frustratingly, it was too late to go down to the surgical wards now. Lunch would be arriving at any minute and doctors would definitely be persona non grata.

Grabbing the notebook in which she kept a private record of all the work she did, Fliss set off for the senior staff common room. There might be some company there, too.

Kate almost knocked her over, flying out of the room just as Fliss came round the door.

'I want to talk to you,' she halted, 'but I've just been called to Casualty. Some idiot's discovered a wasp's nest on the Heath and been stung for his curiosity. I can't think how much cortisone I've pumped into people these last few days!'

54

'I'll be around,' Fliss grinned as her friend, white coat flapping, disappeared down the muggy corridor. It really was very hot; just the sort of weather to make dogs snappy and wasps angry.

She settled herself in one of the low chairs by a window and filled in the details of this morning's operation with Mr Deakin, describing the drugs used, the equipment, all the technical details she would need if she were to have to do the job again, as well as Mr Deakin's comments on possible problems and alternatives. It made impressive reading.

That done, she picked up a medical magazine from the coffee table in front of her—but it was an old one and she had already been through it, learning what she could from it.

Mr Amery came in, settled himself well away from her, and almost immediately dozed off in the heat. Fliss reached for her hanky, in the pocket of her jacket, which she had flung over the arm of the chair. As she pulled the handkerchief clear, a slip of paper fluttered to the floor and she bent to pick it up. It was the competition on the back of the chocolate wrapper that Kate had given her. Fliss scanned the list of prizes. A year's supply of Chewies she could do without, but a crate of champagne or a holiday or a car would be nice. A car; it would certainly be very useful—getting home would be much easier.

She scrabbled around in her bag and found her Biro, but ten minutes later her name and address was all she had managed to fill in. When *had* the first Carachoc bar been produced in England? What was the basic ingredient of chocolate? She had hastily written in *Cocoa* for that one, but she wasn't sure . . .

'Having trouble, Miss Meredith?' Miles away, on a

cocoa plantation in—well, where *did* cocoa grow?—
Fliss looked up vacantly and found Nicholas Da Costa
looking indulgently down on her. He picked up the
notebook she had been filling in and looked at the entry
with today's date. 'You've been busy, I see,' was all he
said.

'Yes, it was a very interesting case,' she said stiffly,
wondering what he wanted. 'Of course, we won't know
how successful it's been for some time, but even if the
child doesn't get full use of the fingers back, at least
they're there, and he's not disfigured.'

'Oh, I'm sure he'll do very well,' Nick said nonchalantly, observing the way that her hair hung smoothly
on her neck, which, despite this recent hot spell, was still
creamy white. She obviously hadn't had time enough for
sunbathing.

'Did your trip to Germany go well?' asked Fliss out of
politeness, aware of his scrutiny and desperate for something to distract his attention.

'You heard about that? Thank goodness it wasn't
supposed to be a secret,' he laughed, and showed her
even white teeth and a surprisingly wide and genuine
smile, which tempted her to respond. Gosh, but he was a
handsome devil when he wasn't going around frowning
people out!

'It was something to do with a ventilation system, I
heard.'

'Yes, I went over with the designer to see what was on
offer over there and work out costs and so on. I'm sure
you know,' he shrugged, as if this was common knowledge and he refused to condescend, 'that in a burns unit
it helps if each patient's air supply—the supply to their
rooms—can be individually controlled and heated and
humidified. And obviously, it's got to be filtered, to keep

things as sterile as humanly possible.'

Fliss nodded knowledgeably and studied his shoes, feeling something suspiciously like a prickle of pleasure and selfconsciousness creep over her at his presence. She should be angry with him for what he had said and done, but grudgingly she admitted that he was probably right to refuse to take on a junior surgeon in the unit and that perhaps she had been reaching too high in her expectations. And on top of that, there was something immensely likeable about this strong, dark man and his positive views. He was direct, knew what he thought, never did things by half, from what she had heard.

'Will you be taking the German system?' She had to look up to ask, and he saw the softening of her clear brown eyes and felt a tingle of more than professional interest. But this was Sir Mortimer's daughter, he reminded himself. Not some innocent young thing, which was what she seemed.

'I think we can do just as well buying over here.' His voice had hardened a little and he took the slightest step back. 'I wanted to let you know that I think I was rather hard on you the other day and that I hope you can accept that what was said was . . .' He rubbed a finger down his long nose, finding it difficult to choose the exact words. 'I meant what I said,' he muttered at last, 'but I didn't intend them to sound quite the way they did.'

'That's all right.' Fliss could have bitten her tongue! How could she accept such an ungracious apology so glibly? How could she pretend that in those few words he had rubbed out all those days of self-recrimination and misery, when she had really begun to wonder whether she could continue her career at Highstead.

'Good,' was all he could think of to say, thinking how ungenerous her acceptance of his apology was. Good lord, did she imagine he made a habit of apologising to junior surgeons whose unrealistic noses had been put out of joint? He was just about to say something more when Peter Locke interrupted them.

'Lunch, Fliss?' He pointedly ignored Mr Da Costa, as the junior doctors, siding with Fliss, had agreed they would.

'Fine.' She jumped to her feet, picked up her bag and turned to go. The chocolate wrapper fluttered unnoticed from her fingers. 'I'll bear what you just said in mind,' she said politely, able now to address him on nearly his own level after five minutes spent contemplating his shoes and legs.

'Do that.' Nick watched the two of them leave, Peter Locke with his arm casually round Fliss's waist as he guided her ahead of him through the door. He had obviously been wrong; there was something between them. Well, that suited him fine, he decided. Something lay on the carpet and he bent his six foot to retrieve it. Nick read the wrapper, smiled, then pocketed it.

'Sorry to disappoint you, but I wasn't just doing my White Knight routine,' Peter announced when they were seated in the dining-room with the best the kitchens could provide in front of them. 'What do you know about the GP course?'

'Not much at all. I suppose my mother might know something,' Fliss said absently. 'Peter, you're not think-ing of . . .' She frowned. 'Why?' Her gentle face showed true concern. The relationship between them might not be the kind to set the world alight, but she understood how vulnerable Peter could be, how sensitive, and no one else seemed to.

'I've been wondering if I ought to go on it. I've felt

more than ever in the last few weeks that anaesthetics doesn't hold much for me.'

'But you're so good,' she protested.

'I have a good record, I know.' He laid down his knife and fork, leant towards her. 'But every time I have a patient with a dicky heart or lungs I'm on edge all through the operation. If I could breathe for them I would! I don't seem to have the sort of toughness that allows me to accept that so long as I've done my best it's all right.'

'You haven't lost a patient this morning, have you?' Fliss asked quietly. Loss of a patient on the table was particularly traumatic for the anaesthetist, who could see, from all his instruments, just what was happening but be powerless to stop it.

'Silly,' he smiled. 'No, I haven't. But I'd like to work on conscious people, have a relationship with them, I think.'

'There are life and death situations in a GP's job, too,' Fliss reminded him. Her mother was a GP—had been for nearly twenty years—and Fliss had grown up in a household where it was taken for granted that either Mum or Dad might not be down for breakfast in the morning, having been called out to an urgent case in the night. 'And with the NHS cut-backs it's even tougher to provide a good service.'

'I know,' sighed Peter melodramatically. 'Thanks for being here, just to let me talk to you. Will you be at home this evening?'

'Yes, come up and let's discuss it all properly.'

'You're a pal, Fliss.' He touched her hand gently as he got to his feet and left. Fliss quietly finished her lunch, her thoughts turning over slowly—and rather sadly.

*   *   *

Though lunch was over on Women's Surgical, the smell of cottage pie remained, savoury and slightly dubious, on the air. Even though all the windows were wide open it was sweltering and the occupants of the beds hoped loudly and frequently for the thunderstorm that seemed imminent.

'Mrs Morrissey, you're a credit to us all,' Fliss smiled at the woman who lay, perspiring gently, on her covers. 'Despite all the problems you're doing as well as someone half your age could be expected to. Look at that, Sister,' she stood back to allow Sister Slater, immaculate as always, despite the tropical temperatures, to look at Mrs Morrissey's double scar, which was healing into a puckered pink line.

'Very nice,' Sister agreed. 'And Mrs Morrissey's been taking solids for twenty-four hours now. Could we dispense with the naso-gastric tube?'

'I was just going to suggest that myself,' said Fliss, obviously pleased with the patient. 'What's the aspirate like?'

Sister held up a specimen jar. 'That's this morning's. We've done the usual acid tests and it's fine.' She showed Fliss the chart.

'How about the pain, Mrs Morrissey? Any problems?'

'No, it's been marvellous, dear,' the patient said emphatically. 'It hurt the first couple of days, but my stitches don't even pull now and I've been out for a walk several times.'

Fliss nodded. 'Well done!' she smiled. 'Now we'll have the tube out as soon as Sister's got a spare moment and concentrate on building up your strength. Honestly, Mrs Morrissey, you're doing very well indeed.'

'Thank you for all your work and care,' Mrs Morrissey blushed. 'And you, Sister. All I'm doing is lying here and following your instructions!'

Fliss signed for the treatment and moved on to Miss Pope, who had entered into deadly rivalry with Mrs Hudd to see who could recover and be discharged first.

'It hasn't done much for the general atmosphere of the ward,' Sister Slater looked reprovingly at the tall young surgeon by her side, 'but Miss Pope's been doing her physiotherapy exercises as if she's in training for the Olympics, so we'll have her out quickly. Poor Mrs Hudd hasn't got a chance, of course, of beating her—she's older and less strong in every way. But even she's doing better than could be expected because of the competition.'

'Mind over matter,' Fliss said smugly. 'It can work, I knew it!'

And five minutes later she was able to deliver the good news to Miss Pope that her stitches could come out in a couple of days' time, followed by her discharge.

'Well, I'm pleased to have triumphed,' said Miss Pope as proudly as if she'd just received a medal, 'though I shall miss the stimulation of the ward—and especially poor Mrs Hudd, of course.' Mrs Hudd sat in her bed opposite and glowered.

'You'll be meeting in Outpatients for your six-week check, so don't let things slide,' Fliss warned mock-sternly. 'Mrs Hudd could still beat you over the longer distance, you know.'

'Did you hear that, Betty?' Miss Pope called cheerfully across the ward. Mrs Hudd nodded vigorously, lay back and proceeded to raise her legs rhythmically, as taught by the physiotherapist.

'We'll be having Jane Fonda workouts next week!' Sister raised her eyes heavenwards.

It was half past four. Fliss had been down to see Alfred Emerson, who was getting along nicely, even without her help, had a quick look in at the Reverend Mr Rose, although she had not ventured to examine him, of course, and had just got back to the senior sitting-room after a trip to Men's Medical to decide whether an ulcer case who was being treated medically was suitable for surgery. He had been, and now she sat in one of the work bays provided and filled out the appropriate forms for Barney to sign to arrange the transfer.

It was quiet. Many of those doctors and surgeons who had completed their clinics and lists had gone home; it was too hot to hang around. Fliss decided to finish what she was doing, have a quick peep into the children's ward to see how her patient of this morning was going on, and then head for home and a cold shower. She was beginning to feel like a shammy leather wrung out in tepid water.

The telephone interrupted her plans suddenly, though.

'Felicity Meredith,' she answered it. It was an internal call from Casualty. Was there anyone in the surgeons' room who could come right away to see a patient brought in with major abrasions of the face?

'I'm on my way,' she said calmly, clipped all her papers to her board and dashed off to Casualty.

'I'm sorry to call you out,' the duty officer, Andy Lee again, apologised as he led Fliss through the tiny area of Outpatients cordoned off for use as a casualty waiting area and rarely occupied. 'This chap's been through a windscreen and we need someone good with sutures to have a look at him. If it's too difficult we can always pack him off to Bart's . . .'

'A windscreen? We haven't had one of those for ages,

not since seat-belt laws. What happened?' she asked, pausing outside the cubicle.

'He was on a newspaper round—you know, from the printers, out of a van. The van stops outside a shop, he dashes in with a bale of evening papers, jumps back inside the van again and they're off. He's exempt from the law because having to stop to put a seat-belt on each time would slow him down and stop him doing his job properly,' Andy explained. 'This time he jumps in, driver pulls out into the traffic and wham! into a taxi. The driver's okay, but the delivery boy's out through the window.'

Fliss braced herself for the worst—and indeed, the patient was in a very bad state, with glass embedded in a dozen cuts across his nose and lips and up into his hairline.

'Can you do it?' asked Andy anxiously.

'Yes. What's he had?' she asked, checking the medication. And within twenty minutes, for the second time in a few days, she found herself working with a scratch theatre team on an unexpected case.

'We'll need a variety of suture packs,' she instructed the theatre nurse. 'Plenty of medium fine silk, something a bit heavier for the nose . . .'

She had been working for more than an hour, removing each sliver of glass, irrigating the wounds, using a head lamp and magnifier to put in the smallest, neatest stitches possible, when there was the sound of someone else washing up in the scrub room. Fliss ignored it, gently preparing her suture pattern to draw the cut bottom lip back into place. Deep in concentration, pausing only to request a needle-holder or a different sized suture from the nurse, she took no notice as a figure approached, gowned and gloved and masked and stopped at her side.

Holding her breath, she drew the fine filaments together and the boy's torn lip closed neatly, absolutely in line.

'Would you like me to take over?' Tying the threads in a deft, one-handed knot that showed her skill, Fliss looked sharply up at Nick Da Costa.

'It's going fine,' she said coolly. 'I've just got this gash on the chin to close up, and the cut on his forehead might need a stitch, but it won't take long.'

'I'll watch,' Nicholas Da Costa announced. 'I need to keep my hand in.' The theatre nurse looked admiringly across to him, but already Miss Meredith was back at the job, easing swollen skin and flesh back into position with gentle fingers, finding just the right amount of tension to hold it in place without puckering or straining the surrounding areas. She seemed to have a natural ability to persuade it into gentle alignment, and infinite patience.

All this Nick noticed, and when he motioned Fliss aside and inserted two stitches into the chin laceration and drew them up with practised speed, she was in a position to appreciate his skill, too.

'You're very fast,' she said, unwilling to praise him when it was already obvious that he knew just how good he was. 'But then you've had years' more practice than I have.'

His eyes crinkled over the mask. Trust a Meredith not to eulogise about a neat piece of work! It was the first time he had seen her in theatre gear, those earnest eyes glowing valiantly in the blueish light, that broad sweep of forehead visible now that her hair was pulled back under the unbecoming theatre cap. It pleased him, somehow, that she wasn't a beauty. If she had been, he would have felt honour bound to have his revenge by seducing Sir Mortimer's daughter and making her love him, and then leaving her high and dry. That was a form of action that Sir Mortimer, bluff and middle-aged, could never emulate.

He found himself staring, captivated, at Fliss's deft fingers as she completed the final touches of the procedure, covering the wounds with tulle gras. She wasn't so bad-looking, was she? There was a certain innocent charm about her—a girlish quality that intrigued him. It would be interesting to find out just how tough she really was . . . In that instant he made his mind up.

Fliss dawdled as long as she could, writing up the notes, filling in Trevor's records, speaking to his anxious mother, who had turned up on hearing of the accident. In the back of her mind she wanted to avoid Nicholas Da Costa—not, for once, because he had been rude or they had parted on less than friendly terms, but because there was something about the man that got under her skin. He left her feeling the need for his approval, something she had never known before, not even as a student, for she had always come up to scratch and been told so. And because he didn't praise her or assure her that she was doing well, Fliss felt rattled—and angry with herself, too, because she was quite aware of how irrational it all was.

As she stepped out of the lift and into Reception, the change in the air hit her—it must have rained, for suddenly the humidity had gone and the temperature dropped; and so did her tension and irritation. Huge blobs of rain were still falling on to the car park, which, judging by its puddles, must already have been drenched. A small crowd of people were already standing by the door waiting for taxis. Fliss, suddenly lighthearted, decided that rain or no rain, umbrella or no, she would walk home.

The people in Reception smiled longingly as she folded her jacket into the bag she carried and stepped out into the shower. Within seconds her blouse was plastered to her skin and her hair in its ponytail had begun to drip. But Fliss raised her face to the skies as she walked, feeling the cooling downpour, stretching her neck to receive it.

Nick Da Costa put his navy BMW into gear and cruised slowly along to her side. For a few moments she didn't seem to realise he was there; she had a useful habit of being able to cut herself off for a while from the real world, and she had done it now. He wound down his window.

'Does it feel good?' Her smile, so serene, as she turned to him made him grin back.

'Wonderful!' Nick could barely raise his eyes from where her blouse had adhered to her body; her bra, so substantial this morning, was transparent now and she was almost naked before his eyes. If his idea had wavered while he waited for her to emerge from the hospital, it was reinforced now. Seducing Fliss Meredith would not necessarily be just an effective way of teaching her a lesson—it would be thoroughly enjoyable.

'I'd like to give you a lift—before you find yourself in trouble.' He nodded casually towards her see-through blouse and opened the car door for her, glad that she couldn't sense the quickened race of his heart.

'Oh!' Fliss instinctively held her bag across herself. 'But I'll ruin your upholstery.' Oh, what a stupid idea this was, she thought inwardly.

'We can fix that—if you don't mind a few dog hairs.'

From the rear seat he took an old plaid rug and covered the passenger seat for her. Before she was really sure of what she was doing, Fliss was seated and Nicholas Da Costa was enquiring about the way to her home. He didn't seem to be any more impressed by her half-naked display than he had been by her skills as a surgeon, for he drove swiftly and with the minimum of fuss to her front door.

As Fliss was struggling with the door catch and saying embarrassed thank-yous, while trying at the same time not to reveal too much of herself to his view, Jane came tripping up the road, umbrella in hand. She gave a friendly wave as she saw Fliss—and an obvious double-take as Nicholas Da Costa emerged from the other side of the car.

'Hello,' she chirped, and the word held a wealth of meaning, including, 'Who's this, then?', 'Aren't you going to introduce us?' and, 'How on earth did *you* manage this?'

'This is Nicholas Da Costa, the head of the Seymour unit. I *told* you about him, I think.' Fliss delivered the last with an agonised look that begged Jane to be tactful. 'And this is Jane, who has the flat above me.'

'I wondered if I could be a nuisance and use the telephone?' Nick asked smoothly, addressing himself to Jane, who had already developed an attractive pout.

'Of course—but why not use Fliss's? How about some tea, Fliss—you make better tea than I do,' she suggested.

'That would be lovely,' Nick jumped in before Fliss, whose face was growing ever blacker, could refuse. They went into the house and Fliss fumbled for her keys. It was difficult, trying to unlock a door with a large bag clutched to one's bosom.

'Allow me.' Mr Da Costa took the Yale key, flicked it in the lock and opened the door for them to enter. Within moments, it seemed, he and Jane had made themselves comfortable on the sofa and were in deep conversation about America, where Jane had recently been on a business trip. As Fliss filled the kettle in the kitchen she heard her friend's trill of laughter at some mild witticism delivered by Nick Da Costa, and knew he was getting the works. Well, she thumped about crossly, serve him right!

In her bedroom she stripped out of her blouse and skirt and everything beneath it and pulled on her faded Levi's and a light sweatshirt. He needn't think she was going to dress up for him. Her hair, rubbed roughly under the drier for a few minutes, responded by fluffing up softly and looking better than it did after an hour's careful attention, and her skin glowed from its assault by the rain.

Barefoot she returned to the sitting-room, to discover that Jane had been upstairs to fetch her photos and that she and Nick were sitting side by side on the chintz sofa laughing over them. They barely looked up at Fliss's arrival, so engrossed in something or other were they, and she stamped back to the kitchen in agitation, stubbing her toe on the way. The kettle had boiled and she made tea. Three mugs were arranged on the tray; not her best china by far, but oh, so appropriate. There was one labelled *Arsenic* for Nicholas Da Costa, a rather precious Mabel Lucie Attwell one for Jane, which portrayed a naughty little girl in rather twee fashion, and her mother's Coronation mug for Fliss.

Chucking a packet of chocolate digestives on to a plate, Fliss presented the tray to her guests. Nick Da Costa raised his mug, read the slogan and raised his

eyebrows too. 'Chocolate biscuits,' he said appreciat-
ively, taking two. 'I adore chocolate. I remember the
first Carachoc Bar being introduced in 1969.' He looked
blandly at Fliss, only the tiniest twitch at the corner of his
handsome mouth indicating his amusement.

Jane seemed unimpressed by this knowledge and
quickly dragged him back into a debate on the delights of
San Francisco. Was he bored? Fliss thought his eyes
glazed slightly at the non-stop chatter, all aimed at
massaging his ego, but she couldn't be sure. Feet tucked
under her, her slim-hipped figure shown to its best
advantage in jeans, she sat in her armchair, an outsider
in her own home, and watched her visitors.

Her thoughts must have drifted for a moment, for the
next thing she knew, Nick was on his feet and preparing
to leave. Fliss jumped up and went to escort him out, but
he bent to the tray and picked up a couple more biscuits.
'For the journey home,' he explained, a wicked gleam in
his eye. 'Don't want my blood sugar to run too low.'

Jane gazed rapturously at his back as he went into the
hallway; Fliss could see her drooling over him over his
shoulder. Quietly, with brief thanks for the lift, she let
him out of the front door. He walked down the overgrown path without a word, but as he got to the end he
raised a hand—didn't turn, just saluted her briefly as if
he knew she would still be there watching him go.
Without warning her heart flipped; though they had said
barely a word to each other a barrier seemed to have
been broken down. He had seen her home and her work;
they were no longer strangers brought together by
circumstances beyond their control.

'My God—he's *gorgeous*! Why don't you like him? Oh,
Fliss, you must be mad!' Jane was in raptures on the

sofa. Only now that Nick had gone did she allow herself
to indulge in a chocolate biscuit—she didn't want him to
think she was the kind of girl who pigged biscuits.

'He's also ruthless—and I should warn you, Jane, he's
been at the hospital a week and he's already loved and
left a couple of nurses. Think about him by all means,
but don't have anything to do with him.' Fliss wagged
a maternal finger.

'Too late,' sighed Jane, reclining on the much used
cushions. 'I'm going out with him on Thursday night—
and anyway, I'm already in love with him.'

Fliss pulled a resigned face and took the mugs back
into the kitchen. She ran some water, added washing-up
liquid and stood there with her hands in the mixture, too
hurt to do more. Her thoughts wouldn't come straight;
no matter how much she tried to sort them out they
remained a tangled mess. But what she was sure of was a
sense of betrayal and a thud of sickness deep down.

'You're very quiet!' Jane skipped round the kitchen
door and registered the look on her friend's face. 'Oh,
Fliss! You're not . . . You didn't have your eye on him
yourself, did you? I'll go and call it off now if you
did . . .'

'Don't be silly.' Fliss wiped a bubbly hand across her
nose and sniffed. 'I wouldn't touch him if you paid me.
But do, please, be careful.'

CHAPTER FOUR

THE honey-coloured stone of the tiny country station glowed in the late morning sun as Fliss clambered out on to the platform and breathed the Cotswold air. From farther down the platform, by the ticket office, there came a shriek.

'Mummy! Biddy! There's Fliss!' And then Matthew came pounding down the platform to greet her, all lolloping arms and legs and his tongue sticking out in abandon. A couple who had also just alighted turned to watch curiously—and then turned away in embarrassment as they realised that this ten-year-old boy was not 'quite as he should be.'

'Hello, love!' Fliss opened her arms wide and tried to put them round him, but he was already so big it was rather a job. He hugged her as if he hadn't seen her for years and planted a slobbering but definitely loving kiss on her cheek, his slanted eyes shining with joy. For Matt had been born many years after Fliss, at a time of their mother's life when another child was definitely not expected and before sophisticated tests had been able to diagnose Down's Syndrome before birth.

Not that anyone in the Meredith family made any bones about that. Matthew, despite all the problems, was a perpetual joy; so sunny and uncomplicated and undemanding that he was a sought-after companion.

'When did school break up?' asked Fliss, allowing him to carry her bag. He walked importantly off with her, his arm through hers, doing his perfect gentleman act, a riotous grin on his face.

'Two weeks,' he said thickly. He spent term-time as a weekly boarder at a splendid school just outside Oxford and rather resented the holidays, when he was separated from his friends.

'Hello, darling. It's lovely to see you.' Mrs Meredith, tall and strong-featured but with the same natural elegance her daughter had inherited, stepped forward to kiss Fliss's cheek. 'Biddy's here too, back at the car. We've been shopping, haven't we, Matt?'

'I've got new socks,' he agreed, and led them through the ticket barrier where the collector smiled broadly at Fliss and her family and enquired about what she'd been up to recently. It was so nice, she thought, to come home to a place where everyone seemed to know you and be interested in what you'd been doing; not at all like London, where you could go days without a friendly word.

Biddy, a large, motherly lady in her early sixties, sat in the back seat of the large estate car and greeted Fliss with all the affection of her real mother. 'You look worn out,' she chided. 'What do they do with you down there, eh? Matthew, you come and sit in the back with me, love.' He climbed obediently in, setting down Fliss's overnight case with great care and concern for its contents, and snuggled up to Biddy.'

'I like it when Fliss comes home,' was all he had to say.

'I hope you didn't expect to have a quiet couple of days' rest,' Mrs Meredith smiled at her daughter as she finished her raspberries and cream and lay back in her garden chair to lap up the sun. The trees rustled softly in the wind and bees hummed around the honeysuckle and magnolia. 'I haven't told Matthew yet because I knew he'd get over-excited, but Jill Crashaw's expecting you for a riding lesson this afternoon, and tonight we're all going to see the local Am Dram's version of *The Sound of Music*, with an invitation to the Goughs' for supper afterwards.'

'It'll be nice to see David Gough again,' Fliss drowsily rubbed her eyes. 'I haven't seen him since we were at school, years ago. When did Matt start riding?'

'A couple of months ago, with the school. Didn't he write and tell you all about it?'

'He did say something about a horse, but what with his writing and his vivid imagination, I didn't realise he meant he'd been riding it!' Fliss chuckled. 'Will you be coming to watch us?'

Mrs Meredith shook her head. 'I'm on duty this afternoon and I'm expecting to be called out. The Mayburys' mother is very ill. She's nearly ninety and just very, very tired. I didn't expect her to get through last night, to be honest, so I'd like to be here if I'm needed this afternoon.'

'Does it make you sad to have to deal with this sort of thing?' Fliss sat up, thoughts of Peter running through her head.

'Sad, yes, but also rather privileged to be so trusted by people.' Sheila Meredith's calm brown eyes studied her daughter's concerned face. 'The only thing we can be sure of is that at some time or other we're going to come to the end of our lives; I like to feel that I can help people approach it with all the dignity and acceptance possible. And,' she laughed warningly, 'don't let's get too gloomy. I have my fair share of births and cures too, you know! You surgeons, you're all the same—you think you do it all!'

The sight of Matthew, hard hat awry, tongue poking out of his mouth in concentration, trotting confidently around Jill Crashaw's paddock, made Fliss's day. After the initial warm-up all three of them went for a hack around the woods, Matt confidently leading the way on his stalwart pony, who knew the route better than any of the humans. All her worries fled Fliss's head, as they always did when she came home.

How could she think of the hospital and all the things that went with it when there was such a super production of *The Sound of Music* to enjoy? 'I haven't laughed so much for a long time,' she confessed to one of the neighbours who had also turned up at the Goughs'. 'Even during the sad bits; aren't there any local men who can sing?'

Matthew, who was treated just as any other ten-year-old by those who knew him, was out at the back of the Goughs' lovely stone house with other children and came tearing back to announce that the doe had had babies—and he wanted one.

'And who's going to look after it when you're at school?' Fliss asked.

'Biddy will,' said Matt certainly. 'She used to look after my guinea-pig.'

Poor Biddy, Fliss thought wryly. Had she known what she was letting herself in for when she'd come to the family eighteen years ago as a housekeeper? Though she had her own cottage in the village she seemed to have become indispensable to the Merediths—and they, in a way, to her.

Sunday morning passed sedately, with breakfast in the garden and the newspapers read at leisure in the sunshine. Fliss dozed, helped wash up, went fishing with Matt in the stream at the end of the garden, read the letters her father had sent from his latest trip to round out the brief postcards she'd received from him, and felt her strength and serenity return. How wonderful it would be to stay for a week—or a month . . .

But at ten to six they were all waiting on the platform for the London train, Fliss with a sunburned nose and shoulders, cold roast beef in her bag and a huge bunch of flowers in her arms. The signal indicating the arrival of the train flapped up and Matt went into raptures. Biddy enveloped her in her plump arms and told her to be good, and Mrs Meredith, having kissed her daughter, drew her aside.

'I was wondering about coming up to London for Matt's birthday. We could take him along to see Dr Thomas in the morning, just to get his check-up done, and then have an afternoon out together. Would you be able to take an afternoon off?'

'Try stopping me,' Fliss said firmly. 'In fact, come back to the flat afterwards and have tea with me. I'll make Matt a birthday cake!'

'How could I refuse such an offer!' The train pulled in, and with a last glance at the glorious countryside and her smiling family, Fliss opened the door, climbed in, and waved goodbye to them.

Relaxed, cheerful and with thoughts of Nicholas Da Costa cordoned off firmly at the back of her mind, Fliss bounced up the steps and into Outpatients on Monday morning. The cleaners were just finishing the floor and all was deceptively quiet and calm. It was only just eight-thirty and there were few people around.

Minding the wet tiles underfoot—no point in antagonising the cleaning staff—she picked her way through to the medical offices. With a big clinic this morning Barney ought to be in soon. But he wasn't in his room, damn him—and he wasn't in the sitting-room, or the dining-room, where Fliss went to get a cup of coffee. Nick Da Costa was, though, and he was deep in conversation with Mr Amery about something. The two of them sat together sketching something on the tabletop with their fingers and Fliss was able to watch.

Mr Amery was in his usual shapeless blue suit that must have been purchased secondhand from Oxfam several years ago. Nick was in a fine blue and white shirt that positively glowed against his tanned, saturnine good looks. Fliss didn't know much about men's clothes—not much about men at all really, except how their bodies worked—but she'd read fashion magazines in her time and was quite prepared to swear that Mr Da Costa's slim tie was silk and his silver-grey trousers cut expensively. Just as she was pricing his shoes he glanced up and saw her, and cast a brief uninterested nod in her direction.

She had seen little of him, except at a distance, for days. He had called at the house on Thursday to pick up Jane, she knew, because she had just happened to be watching out of the front window when he had pulled up in the car; and she had then dropped down behind the sofa so that he didn't see her as he came up the garden path.

Jane had come back well into the small hours and had sung *Some Enchanted Evening* all the way up the stairs and into her own flat. Fliss could only presume that Nicholas Da Costa had proved true to form, but she secretly dreaded the day when Jane was dropped, as all the others had been. She hoped Jane wouldn't blame *her* for introducing them; after all, she *had* been warned. Fliss had an uncomfortable feeling inside that her motives in warning Jane off had rather more to them than simple friendship.

'Here you are—I tried phoning you last night, but—'

'I went away for the weekend,' Fliss supplied. 'What's up?'

Sue Pickton, the firm's secretary, was a comely young woman in her late twenties, bosomy, round-hipped and either a gorgeous armful or overweight, depending on who was describing her. Right now her blonde curls bobbed agitatedly as she clutched an armful of files and papers to her ample figure.

'It's Mr Morton,' she wailed quietly, 'he's had an accident!'

'When? Is it bad?' Fliss's mind began to reel—no Nigel to take over and a full clinic this morning, and twelve patients being admitted for operations over the next two days . . . Oh lord, what on earth was she going to do?

'He's in the private clinic, the one he works in in Harrow. He's done something to his knee—can't move, so they said when they called yesterday. He's having an operation this morning.' She glanced at the wobbling stack of paperwork. 'You're going to have to do this morning on your own.'

Fliss gulped and nodded. 'But what about the list?'

'I dare say someone'll be able to cover,' said Sue without much conviction. 'I'm off to see what can be done now. I don't suppose you know when Nigel's due back?'

'Middle of next week,' Fliss said absently, already beginning to divide incoming patients into urgent and non-urgent cases in her head. They could send home seven, she reckoned, if necessary—but she'd hate to do it after they'd geared themselves up for the knife. 'I'd best get down to Outpatients and make a start, I suppose.'

It was a long morning, but it seemed to fly by. Nearly all today's appointments were gastro-intestinal cases, most of them fairly similar and for common enough complaints. Fliss didn't feel at all out of her depth; indeed, with Barney away, she seemed to be able to get through things that much more quickly.

With the last patient seen, she picked up her things and almost ran down the corridor to Sue's office.

'Right, what's the situation?' she asked. 'And what's Barney's number? I ought to ring him, I suppose.'

'I rang about twenty minutes ago,' Sue said calmly. 'He's only just come around from the anaesthetic, but they say he's doing as well as can be expected.'

'That's very helpful,' snapped Fliss. 'I don't suppose you told them that we're his staff? His *medical* staff, used to the stalling tactics of the nation's nurses?' She caught herself. 'Sorry, Sue. What's happening about today's admissions?'

'Everything's as planned. You can go round this afternoon and get consent forms done and everything. Mr Da Costa has agreed to step in and lead the team,' Sue said smugly. The winsome smile that crossed her lips told Fliss that Sue had spent some time in the great man's company and fallen under his spell.

'Fine.' Fliss gritted her teeth. 'Have you had your lunch yet?' She shook her head. 'Right,' the junior surgeon and sadistically, 'neither have I. So let's get all the notes for this morning's clinic finished, shall we? With any luck we'll have finished by—two-thirty?'

'Potter, Percival: duodenal ulcer, non-urgent. Put him on the bottom of the list. Letter to the GP to confirm it and request continued medical measures, please. And the last one,' Fliss sighed wearily, because it *was* just about two-thirty and she'd had nothing but a cup of coffee since nine, 'is Lacreavy, Hilda. Ulcerative colitis, not yet operable. I suggest we send her off to the dietician for help and get the allergy experts to have a look at her. Letter—'

'—to her GP to the effect,' echoed Sue, her pen flying across the page of her shorthand notebook. 'Right, I'm off for lunch. I'll have these all done by tomorrow lunchtime if you want to come and sign them.'

The door opened and Nick Da Costa's dark head appeared. 'Here you are,' he said, surprised to find them still working. 'I've got half an hour off from my work on the unit, Miss Meredith. Let's go and get some of those consent forms signed now.'

Sue sat upright at her desk and displayed her assets; Fliss slumped.

'It's all right, I'll go and do them later, after . . .'

'I'd like to meet the people I'm to operate on, if you don't mind. I don't know what Mr Morton's attitude was, but I don't believe that surgeons, whatever their status, should ignore their patients while they're conscious.' He was so businesslike, so brisk, that Fliss found it difficult to believe that he was the same man who had pinched chocolate biscuits for his journey home.

'All right,' she sighed, trying to feel some enthusiasm for the job.

'What's happened to the old chap?' Mrs Hudd, deprived of Miss Pope's companionship, leant across her bed to address Fliss, who had just emerged from the curtained cubicle of an appendix patient. 'I didn't have him, did I?' she gestured to Nick Da Costa, writing up his observations more carefully than Barney ever had.

'No,' Fliss whispered conspiratorially. 'Mr Morton's hurt himself. Mr Da Costa's just temporary.'

'More's the pity,' muttered Mrs Hudd. 'Still, don't suppose you're complaining. Would you like to examine me, Doctor?' she called naughtily.

Nick came over, a broad grin splitting his handsome face.

'I'd *like* to examine you . . . Mrs Hudd,' he read the name on her bed head, 'but you don't happen to be Mr Morton's patient. And I wouldn't want to make your surgeon jealous.' He winked broadly.

Fliss admired his touch—just enough of the lad about it to stop him being accused of stuffiness, flattering to the ladies but still in charge. It was a quality many of the top medics lost on their climb. He *was* a bit of a flatterer; a bit of a dandy, too, she decided. Careful of his appearance. She had watched him roll his sleeves up carefully when he went to wash his hands, as if a splash would ruin his shirt. And his watch was so subtly expensive; he had obviously known exactly what sort of impression he wanted to make when he had bought it.

The next patient on the list was a mastectomy. Sister Slater, slightly more vivacious than usual, pulled the curtains around the patient's bed. The woman was in her late thirties, attractive, well made up—just the sort of woman who would worry about the loss of her breast most. Fliss felt a surge of sympathy go through her. Barney always did a radical operation, believing that the more that was removed, the less chance there was of further trouble. He had a good record, too—but the cosmetic effects weren't too pleasing.

'Hello, Mrs Nicholls.' Nick shook hands, then introduced Fliss politely, almost as if she was an equal, not a junior. He talked about the general background of the operation—the removal of the lump, the biopsy which was carried out on the spot, the various courses of action open to them. The woman nodded, but didn't seem to be taking it all in, then co-operated while they examined her.

'Barney prefers the radical operation,' Fliss murmured, drawing Nick aside and feeling something akin to a burning electric shock go through her as she thoughtlessly put her hand on his arm. 'But I know this patient is very frightened about it, so perhaps we could promise something a bit less drastic. Something rather more bearable . . .'

He was giving her such a strange look that Fliss faltered, wondering if she'd said something ridiculous; wondering whether, with her mind half absorbed by thoughts of him, she'd been daydreaming.

'I wouldn't dream of doing a radical mastectomy on *any* woman,' he said at last, a note of disgust in his voice, 'unless it was absolutely necessary.'

He turned back to the bed and began the long procedure of explaining to the patient just what he would try to do. If he had to remove the breast, he promised, he would try to ensure that the skin remained undamaged so that she could have an implant.

'You mean like having a breast enlargement?' Mrs Nicholls looked wonderingly at him.

'Not exactly, but pretty similar. I can't guarantee that you'll want to wear a bikini again,' he told her honestly. 'But there's no reason why you should look on this as the end of the world. You're a very attractive woman.' His eyes raked her appraisingly and Mrs Nicholls blushed slightly. 'A mastectomy doesn't make the slightest bit of difference to your femininity.'

Sister Slater twitched her eyebrows at Fliss, who was

staggered at such unorthodox bedside manners herself. The audacity of the man! And yet it worked, for Mrs Nicholls signed the consent from without any fuss. Fliss fumed; he could wrap just about anybody round his little finger with that easy charm, couldn't he? Everyone except Sir Mortimer Meredith's daughter.

'You'll be wining and dining Mrs Nicholls as soon as she's discharged, I assume?' she growled as they set off to Men's Surgical.

'What's that supposed to mean?' asked Nick icily. 'Are you suggesting that I have adulterous longings for my patient?' His stare was certainly not intended to raise a laugh.

'I hadn't realised it was surgical etiquette to flirt with patients,' Fliss insisted.

'When I know someone is in distress and I know exactly how to alleviate that distress I do it—I don't give a damn for etiquette.' He stopped in the empty corridor and stepped menacingly towards her. Fliss stepped back against the wall, not frightened but fascinated by the way his lips curled, the way his eyes, normally like liquid chocolate, had suddenly darkened to flashing black coals. 'Just because of who you are and what you've done, don't go round assuming that you know better than anyone else. Most of your experience is textbook stuff, Miss Meredith. In the school of real life you wouldn't stand a chance!'

Fliss followed, in silence, to Men's Surgical. She knew she had been unforgivably rude to a senior member of staff, even if he had invited her familiarity. Barney wouldn't have behaved like that, though—nor Mr Amery or any other senior surgeon. But then none of them were quite as sensitive to the needs of the patients or as devilishly attractive as Nicholas Da Costa. She certainly didn't dream about *them* at night!

What was more, she was even prepared to admit, albeit grudgingly, that Nick Da Costa was absolutely right in what he had said. She knew nothing when it came to real life. She had lapped up all she could from her studies, but when it came to a finer knowledge of people and emotions she was hopelessly naïve. All the same, his treatment of Mrs Nicholls *was* questionable, a defiant little voice insisted deep inside. A more mature man would have been able to reassure her without that raking gaze and calculating smile. Damn it, she reminded herself; don't be won round by his occasional charm! He's a womaniser—a brilliant, irresistible, irresponsible womaniser.

She'd met men like him before in passing, but never got to know them. Men in power, men, surgeons some of them, who walked a tightrope at work and didn't want anything serious or demanding to occupy their spare time. Who wanted the release of a physical relationship but none of the emotional drain involved. Their charming act became almost second nature—it dazzled whenever a woman hove into view. But men like that had no real respect for them, they just used them as a means to an end . . .

With such thoughts in mind, they toured the male surgical ward quickly, Fliss answering routine questions about the patients' histories with monosyllabic replies and her eyes fixed demurely downwards. Mr Da Costa made no move to lift the tense atmosphere, for inside he was seething. All right, so it had been a cheap trick to do that to Mrs Nicholls—he'd seen Sister Slater's twitchy eyebrow too, hadn't he? And now here was Felicity Meredith pretending butter wouldn't melt in her mouth—no, he thought sharply, knowing *her* it wouldn't!—and making a display of her disapproval. How the hell was he going to bear the next few days working with Miss Perfect?—right down from her sensible leather shoes to her stylishly unpretentious chintzy sofa . . .

'I've got to get back to a planning meeting,' he growled, thrusting the signed consent forms into her arms and avoiding that steady gaze he had grown to fear. This girl was like a conscience to him; quiet, calm, aware of what was right and wrong, always speaking her mind. Had he ever been like that? Known the books backwards, uncorrupted by the real world and the need to compromise?

'We start at eight tomorrow morning. You'd better arrange it. And make sure you're there on time.' With that injunction, he stalked off. Fliss determined not to follow him, took the opposite direction and found herself in the children's wards.

'Who would you like to see?' A smiling black nurse with a toddler under one arm greeted her.

'I . . .' Fliss was just about to make her excuses when Kate's voice sang out and rescued her from looking foolish.

'Ah, I'm glad you've come up. I told you I wanted to see you, didn't I?' Here on the wards in her white coat, Kate held sway, no longer the amusingly straight-faced feminist of the canteen but a figure of some importance. Her bearing, even her step, was more official. Fliss wondered if the same transformation overcame her on the wards and decided that it did; after all, she was often surprised about how seriously the patients could take her.

'Come and have a look at this.' Kate dragged her down the ward to a cot where a child lay with light bandages over his head. 'Look.' Kate gently unwound them. The child was sleepy, co-operative, aged about eight but behaving rather strangely. Fliss took in the barely visible stitch marks at the eyelids as Kate displayed them, the ears smoothed back with a nip and tuck and the pink scar that showed a gash in his forehead.

'That's what he came in for,' Kate said quietly. 'He's Down's, you know.' Fliss's brow puckered. 'Da Costa sewed him up when he came in, had a chat with his parents and then took him back down to theatre and did his eyes and ears. You didn't need a tongue-bob, did you, Jamie,' she smoothed the child's cheek, 'or he would have done that too.'

'You mean . . . ?' Fliss stared aghast. She'd heard about this happening in the States—but here? Parents anxious to have their Down's children absorbed normally into society sometimes had these minor operations carried out so that the characteristic slit eyes and sticky-out ears and protruding tongue were banished. Irrational revulsion welled up unside her, revulsion born of loyalty to Matt, whose eccentric looks hid a child so lovable that no one in their right mind would reject him. All this cosmetic surgery was so superficial, so unnecessary! It was people's attitudes that needed changing, that was all!

All this she told a shocked Kate in the ward's office after Jamie had been bandaged up again. How dared Da Costa play God! Who did he think he was? Was he so utterly obsessed with the way things looked that he could put an already damaged child through more trauma?

'Fliss!' Kate screeched through the tirade, 'I think it's terrific. I really do. If Jamie's parents can take him out without people staring—and they do, you know, no matter how sympathetic they are—then that's great.'

'And what do we do next? Keep ugly people off the streets so that we don't offend anyone?' Fliss asked coldly. 'How can you, Kate? That man's got to you, just like he's won over everyone else. How could you be so blind? He's brought all his sharp American ways over with him, and you just swallow them whole . . .'

'You're too close to the problem,' Kate said gently. 'I know he wasn't very nice to you and I know you've got Matt, but try to be realistic, will you? Look at it positively; it'll take a while to change the world, but meanwhile Jamie and people like him can have a better life.'

'I agree—particularly with the bit about her being unrealistic.' Nicholas Da Costa stood in the doorway of the adjoining room, the connecting door half open. His eyes swept over Fliss's face, blazing with righteous indignation, and there was a kind of sadness in them. Real sadness at her lack of understanding of the ways of the world, her idealistic stance that opened her to so many blows.

'Do you really think you can solve Jamie's problems with a bit of neat surgery?' she asked, more rational now. 'Seriously, what difference does it make? I'm not saying it's not a good job,' she hastened to add, seeing his eyes cloud. 'But until you've really had something to do with these sort of children . . .'

'But there I have the advantage on you, *again*,' he interrupted smoothly, 'because I do have experience. And you don't.'

'Actually . . .' Kate, caught between them in a conversation with a deeper meaning than she could hope to understand, attempted to come to Fliss's defence. Her friend's reaction had set her thinking a bit, wondering whether she hadn't been a bit hasty in congratulating Mr Da Costa on the achievement as if he'd just sailed the

Atlantic single-handed, and she was determined to have her say.

'Has nothing to do with it,' Nick Da Costa snapped. 'Miss Meredith seems to see herself as a sort of modern-day Joan of Arc and St George rolled into one!'

He put a hand to his head, in real despair. What did this hospital do to attract such women? he wondered as he shut the door gently on them. Well, thank goodness he was seeing Jane tonight. She, at least, wasn't trying to put the world to rights.

CHAPTER FIVE

'How did you do it?' Fliss sat at the end of Barney's bed with his small daughter in her lap. Beth, Barney's long-suffering wife, sat with the new baby cradled in her arms. Roland and Tamsin, rather older, were mucking about in the *en suite* bathroom—it sounded rather as if they were taking a shower and every so often, when their squeaks grew too boisterous, Barney would give a roar that would shut them up for a few minutes.

'Silly domestic accident,' he mumbled incoherently.

'I'd dug out Roland's old skateboard to go to a jumble sale,' Beth piped up in her strangely girlish voice. 'Barney said it was too good to go off to charity and Roly said it was broken, so his father set out to prove that it wasn't—all the way down the rockery steps, didn't you, darling?'

'It's broken now,' young Roland called cheekily from the bathroom. Barney's threatening grunt quieted any further rebellion.

'Oh dear,' Fliss pulled a sympathetic face and tried not to giggle at the thought. 'What's happened, exactly? Sue said you'd torn your knee.'

'Ligaments, the lot. Absolute agony.' The baby wailed and Beth went to put it to her breast. 'Are you sure there aren't any visiting restrictions?' Barney asked warily. 'We're only allowed two to a bed at Highstead, aren't we, Fliss?' It was plain that he was getting fed up with the attentions of his family, who had all been here twenty minutes ago when Fliss arrived. Sympathetic though she was, she had no intention of letting him get off lightly.

'It's one of the little perks of going private, I expect— you know, you're always telling me how wonderful it is. I wouldn't be surprised if there's twenty-four-hour visiting.' Her face was a picture of gloom. 'What's the food like?'

'Better than anything you'll get at Highstead,' he said more brightly. 'But not as good as home.' He held Beth's hand tenderly as she sat there. 'So you're all fixed up with this new chap until Nigel gets back, I hear.'

'That's right. There's no need to worry about a thing. I'm sure he's very good—and you know I'm capable of most of it now, anyway. Though I'll miss your gall bladder radar.'

'What's that?' Tamsin, rather damp and with her cute-cut blonde hair sticking to her photogenically pink cheeks, prodded Fliss with a steel finger.

'Your daddy knows exactly where his patients' gall bladders are,' Fliss muttered uncomfortably, unsure of whether such things were spoken of in polite society.

'What's a gall bladder?' Tamsin answered with another prod.

'Don't do that to Fliss!' Barney and Beth chorused simultaneously.

'Daddy will explain,' said Fliss quickly, passing the buck.

'Thanks very much,' Barney groaned, adjusting the sheets that covered his bed cage. 'I don't want to chuck you all out, but I'm feeling rather tired . . .' The little girl on Fliss's lap scrambled down and under the bed.

Fliss took the hint and stood up, and Beth went into the bathroom to change the baby's nappy. There was a little shriek as she discovered the mess Roland and

Tamsin had made, then the sound of plump little bare calves being smacked.

'I'll call you after tomorrow's surgery; if you'd like to be kept up to date, that is,' Fliss offered.

'If it's a problem, don't bother. Thanks for coming over, Fliss,' Barney smiled, and held up his hand for her to shake. She bade the assorted bodies under the bed goodbye, called to Beth and escaped down the plush corridors of the private clinic. If that was family life, the reason Barney slaved and moonlighted, she wanted none of it, she decided cynically as she escaped into the evening air. No wonder the children were such monsters, though. Beth was always busy minding the latest arrival and Barney was never around.

On the tube back to Highstead Fliss mulled over her day—a disaster by anyone's accounting. The fact that she had hardly had anything to eat didn't help her view things more roundly, either. But knowing that she had to face Nicholas Da Costa the next morning was like going knowingly to torture. In a way she quite wanted to work with him because the surgeon part of her knew that he was good and she could learn a great deal. But after this afternoon . . . She sighed so deeply that the woman sitting opposite her in the underground carriage got up and moved away, probably under the impression that Fliss had been glue-sniffing.

That sad, hurt look he had given both of them as he had shut the door on them had touched her deeper than anything he had said or done. It was if he really cared in some way; that he regretted the way things had turned out. But he was wrong, of course. If only he'd given her the opportunity to tell him about Matt and put him straight on a lot of the things he presumed to know about her—then things would have to change. With a leaden weight about her heart, which she ascribed to hunger, she let herself into the house, dosed herself with muesli and, too exhausted even to lie awake worrying, fell deeply asleep.

'Come up. You're welcome.' Jane's eyes, shining in the moonlight, told Nick exactly how welcome he was—quite welcome enough to stay until the morning.

He kissed her again and she clung to him knowingly, aware of just what to do to excite a man. But Nick couldn't relax, not here. Not knowing that just a few yards away Felicity Meredith was probably waiting to pounce and accuse him of seducing her friend. Seducing her? He deftly removed Jane's hand from his trouser pocket and pecked her on the cheek, distracted.

'Must go—got a busy list tomorrow,' he murmured, anxious to escape before the lights went on downstairs and Fliss, in flannel probably, came at him like a Valkyrie. 'When shall I see you again, darling?' Even to his own ears he didn't sound very passionate.

'Who cares? Look, Nick,' Jane drew back from him and crossed her arms over her bosom, 'why don't you ask Fliss out? All evening I've had nothing but Master-mind about Felicity Meredith—when's her birthday and who does she go on holiday with and does she go out with Peter . . . When you've got over her, you can call me—and *maybe* I'll come out with you!'

She opened the front door with amazing ease and slammed it behind her. Nick stormed to the end of the garden, wrenched his car door open and flung it shut with a crack that must have roused the whole terrace and done nothing for its hinges. He revved up in classic teenage style and, lights glaring and cassette recorder blaring *Homeward Bound*, drove off.

Fliss, woken by the roar, sat bolt upright in bed and listened, her breasts heaving with the surprise of such a rude awakening. She was not wearing flannel, though her cotton T-shirt was not from Janet Reger. Only one set of footsteps ascended the stairs; and Jane banged the door of her flat and clumped around noisily.

Fliss smiled to herself, a secret, rather malicious sort of smile. Casanova had obviously been thwarted by her upright friend. It would do him good to know that not every woman folded at the knees when he came into view. With a gentle chuckle she lay down again and slept.

'Fiona Nicholls. Blood group AB. Excision and biopsy of tumour, right breast.' Peter and the theatre assistant checked off details and the unscrubbed assistant arranged Mrs Nicholls in position, her arm out at an angle on a special board that slotted into the table.

Fliss took a quick breather. She had been hard at it this morning; they had already done a lobectomy, a hiatus hernia and an unexpected hysterectomy which couldn't wait for the gynae list. What was more, Nick Da Costa had let her get on with them, giving quiet advice but acting the assistant himself, holding back obstructions and clamping arteries. Fliss found herself in the unusual position of being in charge—and rose to the occasion admirably. There had been a sticky moment as she had made her dissection into the medial wall of the duodenum and had found that the angle was wrong—but Mr Da Costa was quick to show how the problem could be averted. Looking up quickly as she had proceeded with the operation, she found his eyes twinkling gently over the mask as if he was amused by her steady application, her explanation out loud of every move she

made. Now, for Mrs Nicholls, he took the senior position at the table.

'Are you ready?' he asked Peter. His bedside manner
might be less than textbook, Fliss thought instantly, but
his theatre etiquette was absolutely perfect. Peter
nodded. 'Sister?' Sister McIlvaney purred her response.
Who would have thought that even she could be swayed
by a pair of melting eyes and a display of good manners!

Though the atmosphere in the theatre had been frosty
to begin with it had gradually thawed as they worked,
and Fliss could no more believe now that she had had
an angry confrontation with the man opposite her than
she believed she could fly.

Nick marked the spot with the skin pencil and
explained what he was going to do.

'Mr Morton prefers a radical approach,' Sister said
gently. 'But there's no harm in trying something new, I
dare say.' She turned a grim smile on Nick.

'No harm at all, Sister,' he agreed, taking the scalpel.
'Even someone with your vast experience and knowledge of theatre technique may well find some merit in
this approach.' Sister mumbled something coyly and
made no more comment.

Fliss watched carefully, astonished at the sheer speed
and accuracy with which Nick Da Costa worked. He was
generous to stand beside, allowing her to examine each
stage of the operation, to ask questions. And when the
final dissection had been made he allowed her to sew up,
while he talked about how in hospitals he had worked at
in the past some patients were fitted with an implant at
this stage. His incision had been so well placed, so neat,
that the skin came easily back into alignment, with none
of the ugly dog-ears that sometimes happened.

All in all it had been a remarkably neat and quick

job—and, just as important, it had left the patient with most of her breast intact and a scar which would eventually almost disappear.

'She'll need radiotherapy, of course.' Nick checked the drain that Fliss had just inserted and found that it was good. 'But knowing that she's not disfigured will help her with the strain of the treatment.'

'Preparing a patient psychologically is half the battle,' Fliss agreed as they filled in the details of the operation while waiting for the next patient to be induced and wheeled in.

'Particularly in burns and plastic surgery,' Nick said absently, watching Fliss's firm handwriting and neat expression on the page. 'When you work with people who've been appallingly disfigured or perhaps born with a congenital defect that has hampered their entire lives you've got to be sensitive to their needs. You can't ask them to expect too much—very often a child with a facial disfigurement, for example, will have developed psychological problems because of the way they've been treated all their short life. It's really very difficult not to show revulsion to a kid without a proper nose. I might be able to put the nose right, or at least improve it, but I'd have to be mad to imagine that was the end of the thing.'

Sister and her nurses were setting up the Mayo table, laying out trays carefully for the duodenal ulcer due next, cleaning quickly.

'That's why I did Jamie when he came in.' Fliss looked up, saw that Nick was staring intently at Mr Bowes' operating schedule, which had nothing at all to do with him, Mr Bowes being the veins specialist who worked at Highstead only a couple of times a month. 'His parents were chatting to me, saying how he'd just been rejected from a playgroup, not because he was a problem but because some of the other mothers didn't like the way he looked. It was twenty minutes' work, and it may change not only his life, but his parents', too. No more staring when they go out shopping, no more pitying looks. If you knew what was involved in bringing up a handicapped child, Fliss, you wouldn't have reacted so damningly.'

Fliss remained silent, sensing that he was trying to break through a barrier in their relationship and, peeved with him for his shallow assumptions as she was, curious to know what direction they would now take. As a surgeon she liked him very much, would willingly work with him any time. But as a man? No, it was best to steer clear of men like this—they were only trouble. How on earth can you know about that? a reasonable voice asked inside her. How many men have you known? And how many like this one? She gagged the voice of doubt.

'Come to lunch with me.' Having memorised Mr Bowes' schedule and feeling as gauche as he had at sixteen when he had first suggested something more than a quick peck on the cheek to an equally youthful girl-friend, Nick revolved to face the recurring object of his dreams. What he had seen of Felicity Meredith in the past few days had convinced him that she wasn't quite the monster he had at first imagined. She was cool and calm and methodical, certainly, but not the forbidding career woman he had feared. He still cringed slightly at the memory of her sitting, so serene and collected, opposite him in her flat while he made trivial small talk with the gushing Jane. Fliss's apparent indifference intrigued him; and her quiet confidence today, as she set about her list with skill and without fuss. Perhaps he *had* been hasty in putting her down so rapidly.

'I can't, I'm afraid. I've got a follow-up clinic starting

at one and I'm not likely to finish here much before then.'
Her heart thundered in her breast, but she fixed him with
a clear eye; Nick's first reaction was to laugh the thing
off, as if it had been a joke, for he hadn't received such a
blank refusal for years. But magnanimously he decided
to give her a last chance. 'This evening, then.'

'That would be very nice. I'd like to talk to you about
your work,' she agreed, still hardly effusive. For a
fleeting moment Nick felt regret because he knew that if
the opportunity offered he would go through with his
plan to hit back at Sir Mortimer, and right now he didn't
want to hurt the self-contained Fliss. But why the hell
should he care? he reminded himself. Wasn't she a
self-righteous twig on the family tree? Hadn't she
crossed him, quietly twisted the knife ever since they'd
encountered one another? Home should, he knew, be
indifferent to all this. For God's sake, he was a senior
renowned in his field, the surgical world at his fingertips.
And here was a plain chit of a girl telling him what to do!

The rest of the list was raced through, with barely a
word said. Fliss battled to show that she wasn't upset by
his lack of enthusiasm for their date as he took all the
remaining cases and she was left just to finish and watch.
But all the same, his apparent indifference hurt her
sharply. What on earth had he asked for? she wondered
as yet another patient was wheeled away. And what on
earth had made her accept?

'I'm afraid that this—and this, and this—is no longer
available, sir.' The waiter went regretfully through the
menu but was tactful enough not to tell them that it was
their own fault for being two hours late. Nick's fault,
actually, Fliss thought indignantly. She'd been ready for
him to collect her at eight, as arranged; sitting on the

sofa, biting her nails like a schoolgirl on her first date and dressed up in her best cream jersey dress. And then had come a series of phone calls delaying the time of his arrival. First it was an emergency meeting with the engineers about the Seymour project, then a call to one of the morning's patients . . . Finally, at nearly ten, they had arrived at this discreet French restaurant in High-stead village, only a few minutes down the hill—and it didn't look as if there was much food left for them.

Nick, tired, rather worried at the changes that had to be made to the Seymour, gritted his teeth. This was going to be one hell of an evening.

Fliss helped herself to the crudités, nuts and deep-fried cheese that had been placed on the table as appe-tisers and stared glumly at the menu. Her initial nerves had exhausted her; she didn't know what to make of Mr Da Costa's profound silence—he really seemed to be thinking of other things—and she didn't want the moules marinières or the lamb roasted with garlic that seemed to be all that the restaurant had to offer. Sweetbreads were out, on operating day at least. Her face must have reflected her lack of interest, for Nick said quietly, 'This is a disaster. I don't really want anything on here.'

'Perhaps the lamb . . .'

'I hope you're not seeing patients tomorrow,' he smiled wryly. 'All I need is a good steak, grilled, none of this fancy stuff.'

'Well, if you'd said that earlier, I could have obliged,' Fliss whispered, her mind going to the two rump steaks in her fridge, bought for her dinner with Peter tomorrow.

'Really?' He grinned. 'How do we sneak out?' His smile was infectious and the restraint between them broke.

'I'll go out to get something from the car—I can pretend I've left my hanky in it. And you can go to the gents and climb out of the window. I saw it done on *Minder* just the other week,' she giggled.

'Or it might be easier to own up, buy the waiter a drink from the bar and make a reservation for later in the week at a more reasonable hour. Are you game?' he asked seriously.

'Steak, fresh sweetcorn and salad—nothing fancy,' said Fliss, suddenly nervous at the thought of taking him home—and cooking for him.

'A doctor's meal if I ever heard one,' Nick grinned, watching her fiddle with her napkin. 'Protein, fibre and vitamins. What more could I ask for? Let's go.'

Had she planned it all, things might not have worked out more smoothly. They sat at her little table in the window overlooking the back garden, which was floodlit, as Peter had left his bathroom light on fortuitously. The food was easily cooked and Nick was tired and relaxed and talked gently about what he had been doing on the Seymour unit so far. He seemed to be enjoying himself just lounging on her sofa, examining her china, finding a record to put on her elderly stereo—and he was. Used as he was to leading the conversation, spending his evenings being witty and seductive, it was quite a change for him just to come back to this cosy flat, shabby chintz and all, and have a meal cooked for him. Fliss off duty was shy, retreating to the kitchen when she had the chance, keeping the conversation steadily neutral on topics of work, anxious not to ruin things by talking about Jamie or Mrs Nicholls.

How boring! She panicked quietly in the kitchen, wondering what other more worldly women would do in such a situation. What on earth could he think of her, with her untidy flat and domesticated existence—not at all like Jane or the footloose young nurses he was apparently used to . . . Should she go and sit beside him on the sofa? Make vaguely risqué jokes, as she'd heard Jane do?

In the bathroom Fliss looked at herself in the mirror, the strong features, the general lack of refined sophistication . . . No. He could take her as he found her or not at all.

'Do you see much of your father?' They had finished eating and were having coffee, Nick at ease on the sofa.

'Not a lot. He travels around—oh, you know all this,' she moaned. 'He sends me postcards. This was one of the last ones.' She handed him a picture of Nairobi. 'He's there on a conference, I think.'

Nick turned it casually over, his fingers even longer and stronger looking in the shadowy light. It was date-marked the twenty-sixth of last month; the day that Sir Mortimer had been due to take up his post at Prince-town. Instead of handing it back to her, he stood up slowly and went to place it on the mantelpiece. But instead of returning to the sofa he returned to crouch by the side of Fliss's armchair and took the mug from her hands.

'Look at me,' he said gently. Bemused, half willing something to happen, she did. Those Meredith eyes, shiny with wine and anticipation, locked straight into his. All Nick's experience—and he'd had plenty, even if he wasn't quite the Casanova rumour made out—told him that if he wanted his chance, this was it. Fliss's luminous face regarded his dark cheek with unacknowledged longing; she didn't know what was happening to her, but this sensation was wonderful.

Nick braced himself, silenced his doubts and lowered his mouth to hers, brushing it softly with practised technique, feeling her quiver. And Fliss, gloriously unaware of his cool-hearted intentions, blossomed to her first proper romantic kiss. Her arms came up to cradle him softly to her full breasts, her lips parted and she closed her eyes to feel the delicious sensual shudder go through her.

Nick, eyes open, paused for a moment, thrown by her simple, trusting reaction, and hated himself. And in that split second, with Fliss vulnerable and melting in his arms, her dark eyelashes sweeping his cheek, he felt that same traitorous shudder pass through him; something new, a revelation. Without thought he kissed her again and again, clasped her to him, covered her neck and ears in butterfly kisses, felt a groan rising in his throat. They clung like two people starved, devouring each other, drowning, Fliss totally lost in the whirlpool of new discovery.

There was a bang as the front door slammed and Jane's feet pounded up the stairs, and it was like awakening from a dream—for both of them had guilty associations with Jane.

'I think I'd better go.' Nick was on his feet. 'Don't worry, I can see myself out.' His voice sounded thick and he raked a hand through his tousled hair and bent to pick up his jacket, discarded hours ago. Fliss, still shell-shocked, barely aware of what had happened, watched him leave before she could think to protest and listened to the loud roar of his car as he accelerated into the night.

CHAPTER SIX

NICK climbed the stairs to his temporarily rented flat in an old mansion block on the edge of St John's Wood and let himself in with a sigh. The heavy leather furniture and shiny chrome and smoked glass oppressed him; it was a place for camping out in style—but not like Fliss's homely grotto, full of bric-à-brac and old furniture from home.

The porter had handed him a note on his way in and he sat wearily on the unyielding sofa and read it. It was from one of the nurses on the children's ward, a girl he had gone out with a couple of times. She was pretty, free with her favours but so immature that he had found his mind wandering constantly in her company. Her impassioned pleas that he contact her again, that she had so enjoyed their evenings together, that she was free any time he cared to call . . . He balled it up and threw it into the fireplace.

What on earth had he done? With a sigh Nick held his head in his hands. What was happening to him? If only Fliss hadn't given him that postcard, like a challenge, reminding him of how badly her father had behaved, stirring up suspended thoughts of revenge. And then she had looked at him, those same brown eyes, that serene, Madonna-like stare that made him want to surprise her, shock her . . . There was something more, he knew, but he refused to acknowledge it. Damn it, he thought irritably, now she was bound to fall in love with him like the others, make a nuisance of herself . . . He didn't want to pursue the idea. It was too painfully obvious that he had behaved with complete stupidity. He had a stiff drink to make him sleep and went to bed in the bare, characterless bedroom.

Was it lust or love? Fliss sat in her own cluttered bedroom and regarded her glowing face in her stripped pine mirror. Lust, she decided. For love there had to be compatibility, mutual trust and liking; for lust there simply had to be two physically attracted people and a suitable time and place, which explained this evening's events perfectly.

She felt a flush of gratitude and affection for Mr Da Costa, as well as this awful empty feeling in her stomach. He had shown her what she had been missing through all these years of study and toil; but there was no need for them to ever go any further than that again. What if Jane hadn't come back? she wondered idly, brushing out her hair. What if they hadn't been disturbed, he with uncomfortable memories of his rejection on the doorstep the other night, she with guilty knowledge that she had been eavesdropping? What would they have . . . ? It wasn't even worth contemplating, Fliss told herself crossly. Nothing had happened and nothing would happen. They'd both had a little too much to drink; they were both tired and a little emotional after a day in the operating theatre; that was all. And that was that.

She climbed into bed and lay awake for another hour, looking at the ceiling and feeling a warmth in her body and a traitorous image in the back of her skull. A smile crossed her scrubbed young face. At least he found her attractive enough to interest him, however briefly. With that thought she drifted into sleep.

*   *   *

'Miss Meredith.' Nick Da Costa nodded briefly and set off to do his round, Fliss in tow. He hadn't said a thing about last night, and this morning he had steadfastly refused to look Fliss in the face. Strangely, she didn't feel upset. Oh, there was an ache, a certain sense of deprivation, certainly, but with the naïvety of years of clinical training behind her Fliss just put it down to the fact that she had been alerted to something new which had upset her measured life. Her plans had been put out of synch, her ideas jolted. No wonder she felt subdued! Subdued, but also excited, for now she knew what to expect, she looked forward to a relationship with a man. Nick Da Costa had broken down a barrier—could she be anything but grateful? Not that she wanted to take her friendship with him any further. No, her sensible self insisted; that way lay misery. Better to wait for some-one reliable, faithful, trustworthy . . .

'Mr Da Costa.' She followed to Mrs Nicholls' bedside.

'How do you feel?' asked Nick, checking the patient's heart and casting a practised eye over her BP and temperature chart. 'You've had the pain-killers written up for you, I see.'

'Not too bad at all, Doctor,' the woman sighed. Today, without her make-up and with the natural leth-argy caused by the anaesthetic, Mrs Nicholls was not quite the glamorous creature she had been. If Fliss had felt sympathy before, her heart now went to her as she lay with chest and shoulder bandaged into position. 'Tell me what you did, will you?'

Nick explained the details of the operation, and Fliss watched him admiringly. How lovely it would be to know you had the trust and love of a man like this—a man you could be so proud of, so attractive and capable. There was a twinge of regret around her heart as she silently listed his crimes to herself. His quickness to take against people for no good reason, the grudge he carried against her father, his apparent inability to resist any reasonable-looking woman who crossed his path . . . And then there was his unwillingness to take anyone else's point of view into account, his lack of punctuality—oh no, he would never fit into her life, not in a million years.

Nick, talking quietly to his patient, was aware of Fliss's calm scrutiny and found himself resenting it. How could she be so cool, so couldn't-care-less, when last night she had melted into his arms without a moment's hesitation? A terrible thought veered into his mind. Had she been testing him, seeing how vulnerable he was? Making a fool of him? He realised he had stopped in mid-sentence and drew himself together furiously. Had he seriously ever imagined he could get one up on the Meredith clan?

Alfred Emerson was the last on their list of visits, and it was almost lunchtime by the time Fliss and Nick arrived by the side of his bed. He was out in the main ward, bright, cheerful and pleased to see Fliss.

'Hallo, Doctor darling! Here, look who's come to see me, lads!' he called to his surrounding friends. 'Never thought I'd see you again, not in here, anyway. Not after what happened last time, eh?' He looked across to Nick, who was still refusing to communicate in anything more than monosyllables.

Fliss raised Alfred's gown and had a look at the graft sites, then the donor areas. Sister Walsh stood back quietly—unusually quietly, Fliss thought. She normally insisted on making her presence and her authority felt, reminding Fliss with every word and deed that *she* was in charge of this ward and could do without junior surgeons interfering.

'They're very nice,' she smiled at Alfred. 'What does your wife think about having you home all stripey? Won't be long now, I shouldn't wonder. When's your leg due to come out of plaster?'

''Nother week, they reckon. Here, those patches *are* all going to fade, aren't they? Someone showed me them the other day, held up a mirror so I could see me own bottom! What are things coming to, eh?'

'Give it time, but yes, you should get back pretty much to normal, thanks to Mr Da Costa's quick work,' Fliss said reverently. It hadn't escaped her notice that *his* handiwork was markedly neater than Mr Amery's had been, but she wasn't going to sing his praises, not with him in this bullish mood.

Nick came up and took another look, echoed her words and led her rapidly out into the corridor.

'We have another list tomorrow, I understand?' he asked coldly, still refusing to look her in the face, as if she embarrassed him.

'Yes, tomorrow morning. You've seen most of the patients—mainly hysterectomies and investigations. One for a colostomy, one for gall bladder. Eight in all. You saw five of them on Monday, the others I'll go round this afternoon if you're busy.'

'I am,' he agreed bluntly. 'I'm trying to do two jobs at once, remember? I suppose I can trust you to do them by yourself. Where will you be if I want to see you?' He made the whole thing sound as if it bored him terribly and as if seeing her was the last thing that interested him.

'I'll be with Sue Pickton arranging next month's admissions or on the wards. Have we finished here?' He nodded and walked away as if he had never shared a meal with her, never relaxed on her sofa, never kissed her. Fliss gave a little shrug and went about her own business. Men—would she ever understand them?

'We've got that Mr Farley left over from last month,' Sue said dubiously, watching as Fliss tried to piece together all the admissions for Barney's firm for September. 'Do you remember? He badgered and badgered until he was moved up the list, and then when he got his appointment he announced that he couldn't come in because he was going on holiday.'

'Mmm?' It was like a huge jigsaw, all sky, trying to get this organised. 'Okay, put him in on the seventh. If he can't come in that's too bad, and you have my permission to be as rude as you need to be on the phone.' Fliss surveyed the notes yet again. The schedule would go to the administrators to be verified before the letters went out to the patients.

'That's the best I can do for the time being,' she said quietly. 'We've cleared the urgent list now, have we?' Sue nodded her blonde curls.

'And seventeen off the non-urgents. That's not bad, you know. Our average waiting time is coming down gradually. People moan, you know, but we're not nearly as inefficient as they think.'

Fliss filed the consent forms she'd done straight after lunch, checked over the correspondence and, at half past four, decided she would call it a day. Peter was coming to dinner tonight and she needed to get some more meat. Bidding Sue goodbye, Fliss took her jacket and bag, visited the ladies' and was on her way out when Peter's voice stopped her.

'We need *you*!' He ran to her. 'Anything urgent on? We've just had an emergency peritonitis in and Mr Potter needs an assistant.'

'Sure—though you'll not get any supper at this rate,' Fliss laughed and, taking his proffered arm, trotted with him to theatres. On the way they passed the pigeonholes, and she automatically reached out and removed the leaflets and notes inside hers. Advertising, mostly, and information about forthcoming hospital events. Fliss shoved the wodge into the bottom of her bag and went to get changed.

The patient, when she appeared, was an elderly woman.

'She was brought in this morning for observation,' Mr Potter, one of the older surgeons, explained. 'Went downhill rapidly, though, before she could be added to the schedule.'

Fliss didn't know the Theatre Sister, a young woman, but she smiled at her just the same. Even though one worked in the same environment, there were vast numbers of staff who would be unfamiliar all their working lives.

They waited for Peter to get the patient stable and give the signal for the operation to begin, but he looked worried and seemed to be having difficulty maintaining her life signs.

'This'll have to be quick,' he said at last, his furrowed brow and tense voice expressing more anxiety than his words. 'Her heart's erratic.'

Fliss's mind flew back to what he had said to her not so long ago about flying by the seat of his pants through operations such as these, and she looked up to give him an encouraging nod. But he was already concentrating on the patient's head. Mr Potter, not renowned for his speed, took the scalpel and made his incision, but before they had got under way, Peter's voice rang out again.

'Hold it, please.' The blip of the patient's heartbeat

stabilised again slowly and Peter gave an injection to try to strengthen it before indicating that they could proceed. Fliss, by now beginning to feel the tension herself, stood by with the clamps and diathermy knife. Sister, too, was affected by the atmosphere, for she dropped a swab and gave a muffled apology which was ignored in the silent theatre which resounded to the unnatural pulse of the monitoring equipment.

They had entered the peritoneal cavity and were irrigating it while Mr Potter explored for the source of the problem when the machine let out a piercing tone.

'Cardiac arrest!' Peter was already preparing another injection while the junior nurse ran efficiently to the resus trolley and wheeled it over. Sister had whipped the drapes back and exposed the pale, sadly thin body of the patient, and Fliss, swiftly applying contact gel to the pads on the re-start equipment, placed them both over the patient's breastbone.

'Hands off!' The others stood back and the nurse flicked the switch. Nothing happened. 'Again.' Fliss's voice was grimly calm as the well-rehearsed routine flashed through her mind. But nothing happened this time, or the next two. Mr Potter stood by, ready to reach the heart from inside if necessary, while Fliss started cardiac massage. But she already knew, deep down, that it wasn't going to work. Nothing was going to get this poor elderly lady's heart beating again.

The nurse at Sister's side was counting off the seconds, shouting as each minute passed so that the surgeons knew how long they had to revive the patient. 'Two minutes,' she called above the activity. Three minutes passed, then four, then five. Peter did what he could, using the drugs and gases at his disposal, but all of them knew the inevitable outcome.

'Does she have relatives?' asked Fliss as she closed the site of the operation with as much care as if the patient had fifty years of life ahead of her. Peter, redundant, flipped through the notes in the prep room.

'Nothing here,' he said quietly. His eyes had a sort of glassy, disbelieving look and his mouth was set in a resigned line. Fliss could guess what he was thinking. She had lost a patient before in circumstances not unlike this. It had to happen at some time, she knew. And her mother's words came back as a source of comfort, particularly when she came to fill in the paperwork that always went with something like this. Mrs Elsie Holden had been more than eighty; she tried not to be too callous, but it was hardly a young existence tragically foreshortened.

'I should have foreseen the heart problem,' Peter repeated as they walked home up the hill in the early evening. The sun shone on them and the children play-ing on the Heath and fishing in the ponds. Life went on; Elsie Holden had died, children had starved in the Third World, a political prisoner had been tortured to death— and the traffic crawled up the hill and children on their bicycles still practised their wheelies on the path.

'How on earth could you? And what would you have done if you had?' Fliss said a trifle crossly. 'She *had* to be operated on—you know that. Peter, for goodness' sake, it's sad, but it's not the end of the world!'

He didn't say a thing, but it had obviously affected him deeply. Mr Potter's sympathy, her own pep talk— nothing seemed to placate him.

They bought sausages from the late night corner shop and Fliss, determined not to let the gloom drag her totally down, for she knew she had her own problems to worry about, had an ice-cream too.

'I don't know how you could,' Peter said brittly as they turned towards the house. 'Sometimes I wonder if you're human, you know.'

'I am; I'm very human,' she insisted gently. 'But I'm not all quivering emotion; I allow my head and my heart to work together. If we'd lost a child or a young adult or a breadwinner with a family to support I might have refrained from ice-cream.' She tried to make it sound a little flippant. 'But we've just lost an elderly woman with no known relatives who lived on her own and had a condition that would have killed her anyway. And if you can't survive that, heaven help the next time.'

'There won't be a next time,' Peter said firmly. 'I'm going to give up.'

They had reached the house and Fliss bottled her reply until they were in her flat and Peter was prowling around it. 'I think that's the right decision,' she said firmly.

'You do? No protests about me being such a good anaesthetist?' He seemed shocked, as if she had betrayed him in some way, and suddenly Fliss realised just why they had been friends all this time; not really because they liked each other but because they were useful. Peter had used her to bolster his lack of confidence because he believed that in moments of crisis like this she would always come up with the right answer. Always tell him that he was good, give him the strength to go on. And she had used him to hide behind, to take the heat off her. Except that the heat had never really been on—and now it was, Fliss knew that Peter was useless protection.

For Nicholas Da Costa had come into their lives, and what he represented—whether it was his surgical techniques that showed real concern for his patients or his sexual prowess that liberated the emotions and the body—was like a breath of fresh air in a stale room. Suddenly there was no need to be like Sir Mortimer or Barney, the one so dedicated he had left real life behind, the other trying to fit in too much of everything and making a mess of it all. If Fliss wanted she could have the kind of devil-may-care dedication of Nick Da Costa where etiquette didn't matter so long as the cure did— and where the cure could mean something more than physical well-being.

Peter stared at her, at the slow smile that had begun to creep across her face. 'What's wrong?' he asked.

'Nothing, everything's right. I do think you ought to consider giving up, Peter. You're too sensitive and lacking in confidence to really excel in your field.' There, it had been said. Fliss didn't know what to expect, so she went through to the kitchen and put the sausages on to grill.

'Nobody's ever said that before to me. I've been waiting for years for someone to tell me that so that I could give up with good grace.' His eyes were as wide as hers now. 'All through medical school and interns I was waiting for someone to say, "Locke, your heart isn't really in this, is it?" But they didn't, so I reckoned that perhaps no one really did care that much about it. My family are going to hate it, but I've got it all worked out . . .'

He was like a different person now, almost like a child, full of plans for studying his music full-time and becoming a professional musician. Fliss smiled and poured more of her mother's homemade elderflower champagne into his glass, merely sitting and listening to four years' worth of corked-up aspirations and saying nothing. It grew late; they sat in the shadows, two people who had known each other, been friends with each other for years—and yet knew nothing about each other's hopes and fears. Fliss felt sad that so much seemed to have passed her by. But she wasn't old. All she needed to do was live life to the full and not let it pass her by. She would soon catch up. And perhaps the first thing to do would be to look for a new job. If Nick wouldn't have her on the unit she'd shake herself out of her rut by going elsewhere—abroad, even, where she could do some real good.

When they finally rose from their chairs and Peter turned to go downstairs, he held his arms out to her. With her flat door open a few inches he took her in his arms and gave her a gentle kiss. 'Thanks,' he said with a real smile—one of relief. 'Thanks, Fliss.' He hugged her again with affection.

They were just standing there, almost discovering each other for the first time, when the door of the house opened and Jane and Nicholas Da Costa siphoned into the small hall.

'Hallo! Hallo Fliss, hallo Peter!' Her tone was forced, too bright for comfort. Nick pushed open the door to say hallo properly and found Peter with his arm gently round Fliss's shoulders and both of them looking as if they'd just won the pools or sworn undying love—or both.

He gave them a nod. 'You didn't get my note, then.' It wasn't a question, more an accusation.

'Note?' Fliss was genuinely perplexed.

'I posted a note in your pigeonhole; it's gone, so perhaps someone else took it.' His cold dark eyes made it perfectly clear he did not believe the culprit to be anyone other than Fliss herself.

'Oh, I haven't had time to read my letters. Was it

urgent?' she flustered, aware of his interpretation of the scene before him. Slipping from under Peter's arm, she went to get her bag and the letter to show him that she hadn't yet opened it. But when she got back to the hall he had gone, tugged upstairs by a protesting Jane. Peter, too, was just about to slip away. She said good night to him, shut her door and went back into the sitting room, switching on her anglepoise reading lamp as she went. Nick's note was written on hand-rolled white paper, thick, stylish and rugged, just like his bold black handwriting. Come out to dinner tonight, it read. I want to talk to you seriously about a position in the new Seymour unit which might suit your capabilities. This is not a job offer! He'd underlined the last bit heavily and scrawled his signature at the bottom.

Fliss sat for a long time holding the beautiful paper, just trying to take in all the things that had happened during the day—the heights and depths of emotion and resolution she had experienced. It was too much, it gave her a cold, numbing feeling that she was simply trying to hold too much together and that something was bound to break. Should she, she wondered bleakly, go upstairs and try to explain?

Through the silence of her rooms came the sound of thudding feet and then a womanly giggle. A dark, male voice said something in surprise, and then there was silence, apart from the occasional bump from the bedroom upstairs.

Fliss sat on, feeling quite impossibly alone. She had said goodbye to Peter tonight; goodbye to a man she might once have called a friend and believed it. She had said goodbye, without knowing it, to a job that might have been the one she wanted. She had decided to say goodbye to Highstead and all she knew.

Switching off the light, she put her head in her hands and shed a few silent tears—for Elsie Holden, for herself and for Nick Da Costa upstairs.

MYSTERIOUS SURGEONMYSTERIOUS SURGEONMYSTERIOUS SURGEON

CHAPTER SEVEN

'WHEN will you be free for us to have this chat about the unit?' Fliss had followed Nick into the ante-room and they were both pulling off their gowns and caps prior to taking a shower and changing back into civvies.

'I'm busy today,' he grunted, withdrawing his arms from the sleeves of the gown and revealing a broad expanse of chest encased in a smooth-fitting white T-shirt—a sight that made her innards flip with a kind of breathlessness. 'You'll have to do the post-op follow-ups on your own. There's nothing to worry about, I shouldn't think. I've got a policy meeting to attend and then the building inspector's coming. It'll wait, anyway.'

'I do want the job,' Fliss said quietly. 'I'm not too proud to admit that.' She was too proud, though, to admit that her main reason was the fact that she would be working with a certain Nicholas Da Costa; and too proud to admit to herself that there was something more important in that decision than the fact that he was a superb surgeon. In the intervening twelve hours since his disappearance upstairs with Jane and their somewhat strained conversation after the morning's surgery, Fliss had swung to and fro like the famous swingometer on election night. For five minutes she felt convinced that there could be nothing more exciting, more rewarding, more educational, than working with him—and then there was a conservative backswing that told her that she was guaranteed complete and utter misery by such an arrangement. For what happiness could she hope to

115

have with Nick out every night enjoying himself with a new nurse while she stayed at home and thought about it?

Despite what had happened the other night, she knew he wasn't really attracted to her—not in *that* way. Not plain Felicity Meredith with her plain home cooking and a sofa and a shoulder to cry on. It was self-delusion to imagine that there could ever be anything more than a professional closeness between them—but she was prepared to fight for that, and if being humble was what was required, she would make that sacrifice. He had got over the fact that she was his arch-enemy's daughter, so who knew what else might happen?

'I thought you told me that your plans had changed and that they no longer included working on the unit?' he said, amused, and with a practised movement stripped out his T-shirt. Fliss fixed her eyes firmly on his chin, knowing that if she looked down she would betray her feelings.

'I can change my mind, can't I?' she said defiantly. Her gaze slipped and took in his muscular brown torso and the dark feathering of hair across the chest and arrowing down his abdomen as he pushed the gown and T-shirt into the dirty chute.

Nick's mind was too occupied with the problem in hand to realise that he was being surreptitiously weighed up. He would have been amused and perhaps, unusually, a little embarrassed if he had, for he was having to fight hard to remember that this Joan of Arc-ish female in front of him, all clear skin and shining eyes and soft brown hair, with her mission in life dominating everything she did, was a qualified surgeon—a colleague, a team-mate—and not to be treated as lightly as her featherweight contemporaries, like Jane. Jane's cal-

culating glance had valued his car, his suit, had given him
ratings for the restaurant he took her to and his perform-
ance later in the evening. He was used to it and took such
behaviour with a pinch of salt; women like Jane were
usually ruefully philosophical when he moved on. Fliss
was something quite different.

'Look, I'm going up to see a friend of mine in the
Midlands. He taught me most of the basics of plastic and
cosmetic surgery before I went to the States and he's
doing an operation on Sunday—I'm going to assist
him. Come with me. That way you'll see what it's all
about, then we can discuss it.' He faced her, came a step
closer.

'I'm supposed to be on call,' Fliss frowned, 'but if
you'll put in a word to the head of Surgical Admin I'm
sure we can sort it out.' She looked up to find him only
inches away. She had only to reach out her hand and she
could touch his naked flesh, feel it firm and smooth and
tanned under her fingers. He must do work-outs, she
thought fleetingly, because his pectorals were well developed. If she had had a patient on the table with a
body like this she would have called him vain; but on
Nick Da Costa they were something different. He was so
masculine anyway, so virile-looking . . .

'Okay.' He took a breath that sounded like a little
sigh, and Fliss looked up to see something approaching
an expression of tenderness in his dark eyes. They were
very dark, she thought, medical training coming to the
fore. His pupils were very dilated. Hadn't she read
somewhere that . . .

'In case we don't see each other over the next couple
of days, I'll pick you up early on Sunday morning. Nine,
say. All right?'

'All right,' echoed Fliss. Nick bent slightly and, before

she knew quite what had happened, kissed her gently on the forehead.

'I'll see you,' he said quietly and, as stunned by his unpremeditated action as she was, retreated rapidly to the shower room.

This was all getting out of hand, he told himself as he showered. First he had been crazy enough to leave that note for her, actually suggesting that, despite all he had said, he would consider having her on the new team. And then when, a mere ten minutes later, he had come to his senses and gone back to get it, she had already emptied her pigeonhole.

He turned the thermostat to cold and stood under the freezing spray for several minutes, trying to get things back into perspective. But it was no good, he admitted as he squeezed into his trousers later; it would take something more than a cold shower to get Miss Meredith out of his system. He knew what it was, of course; a single night with her and the magic would be gone, as it had gone from so many other tantalising women. Never before had he hesitated to take what he felt sure he would be offered. But something held him back. Despite her dreadful father and her crusading nature, he liked Felicity Meredith and he wanted to save her from herself. Yes, he repeated sternly, he *liked* her. She made him laugh; he enjoyed working with her; he felt happy being alone with her, just pottering in her home. That was too much to throw away. Besides, she was such an innocent he felt protective. So for both their sakes he'd damn well make sure he behaved himself.

'There we go, Mr Taube. Dr Hinchcliffe'll just put a stitch in there and you'll be as right as rain.'

Although Highstead didn't have a casualty department it did have an outpatients' surgery. And this morning it was Fliss's turn to assist there, instructing some of the younger doctors in the techniques of minor surgery. She had just removed a warty growth from the back of Mr Taube's neck—fairly typical of the kind of job that came in. Some areas of surgery were actually quite suited to outpatient work. Eye surgery, for example, could often be done on such a basis, provided that the patient had someone to care for them on the homeward journey and for the next few days.

This morning she and Simon Hinchcliffe had reduced the tendon sheath of an avid squash fan who had overdone things and had ended up unable to flex his wrist, repaired a minor gynaecological problem, cauterised a nasal polyp . . . All useful things that made life easier for the patients and didn't cause them too much inconvenience.

'This is a prescription for a pain-killer, Mr Taube. You might need it once the anaesthetic has worn-off. Is your wife here? How do you intend getting home?'

'My daughter's here. She'll take me back,' croaked Mr Taube, rather overcome by the stainless steel atmosphere and this brisk young woman who seemed to be telling the doctor what to do. The nurse led him out and Fliss made a note of the prescription on his files.

'Nothing very exciting for you,' she smiled to Simon, who was on secondment from Bart's for a couple of weeks to get some practical experience at something other than his own hospital could offer. He was very goodnatured and helpful with the patients. Fliss didn't doubt that he would make a very good doctor.

'I enjoyed it. It's nice to be able to talk to your patients while you're working, isn't it?' he replied, handing back the final folder while Fliss went to wash her hands. 'Can I take you to the pub for lunch?' he asked diffidently.

''Fraid not. My mother and brother should be waiting for me in Reception right now. It's his birthday and we're off to the Transport Museum or something,' she told him truthfully.

He blushed a little, gave a meaningful, 'Ah,' and, obviously not believing a word of it, made his goodbyes. Fliss dashed down to the staff cloakrooms and in the privacy of the Ladies, slipped into her red trousers and loose T-shirt. Her formal suit she hung carefully inside her locker—it was always useful to keep a spare change of formal and casual clothing at the hospital, she found. If she was called in the night and arrived in jeans, at least she had something suitable to change into if necessary. Not that Highstead's policy on clothes was strict, but she felt that being smart gave her an edge. She might be singled out as being a woman surgeon—but she couldn't be faulted as a scruffy woman surgeon.

Reception was emptying out after the influx of people for Outpatients, but Mrs Meredith and Matt were not to be seen. Fliss hurried along to the surgeons' common room; perhaps someone had seen them and recognised them—because they had visited once or twice in the past and some of the surgeons were acquainted with Sir Mortimer and therefore recognised his wife—but no. Perhaps her mother had driven down and was waiting outside in the car? Fliss ran down the steps and looked round anxiously for the familiar estate car—but could see no sign of it. Mrs Meredith was too accustomed to the ways of hospitals to have given up waiting when Fliss was a few minutes late. Where could she be?

A shout reached Fliss across the tarmac and she looked up. Surely that figure in a yellow construction hat couldn't be Matt? What on earth was he doing sitting on the bulldozer brought in to lay foundations for the Seymour building? She raced across the car park.

'Get down, Matt!' He was already doing so in his anxiety to greet her, and she hoped he wouldn't slip before she got to him.

'What's all the fuss about?' Nick Da Costa emerged from the other side of the vehicle and gave Matt a casual hand down. 'He came out to have a look at the state of the site while Kate took your mother up to Paediatrics.'

'Hallo, lovey! Happy birthday!' Fliss hugged Matt and was hugged firmly back. 'What an amazing hat! What have you been up to, eh? Making the builders work a bit faster?' Nick watched her face, alive with genuine pleasure at seeing her younger brother.

'You didn't tell me about this,' he said darkly above Matt's head, whispering so that the words didn't reach the boy's ears.

'There are an awful lot of things you don't know,' she retorted, a flicker of anger going through her that he, in his own inimitable fashion, should have found out without her having the satisfaction of telling him and wiping that smug look off his face.

'Why has Mum gone to Paediatrics with Kate?' she asked sharply, suddenly taking in what he'd said.

'Dr Meredith has a leukaemia patient in here at the moment, apparently. And there were other things that I dare say she'll find interesting.' There was a note of defence in his voice, as if there were things he would like to say but couldn't.

'We came in a taxi,' Matt said suddenly, breaking the tension. 'Where's my birthday present? Guess what I got from Mum and Dad, Fliss!'

His poor slanted eyes blazed with excitement, and

Fliss gently moved his fingers from his mouth and wiped it while she made deep thinking noises.

'A trail bike?' she suggested, knowing full well that that was what was waiting for him at her flat.

'A horse. Its name is Biggles and it's going to live with Jill Crashaw's other horses,' he managed with fits and starts. His language was as good as it would ever be and he could read a few words laboriously and, given time and a lot of paper to practise on, get his name down legibly. But it was all something of a struggle. Nick looked on compassionately.

'What's that?' asked Matt, pointing to a crane that was swinging a girder into place. His concentration span was very short, no matter how interested he was in anything. Nick explained, telling him uncondescendingly what was going on; how the foundations had been laid, what was going to be built here, and here, as if Matt was as capable of taking in the information as an ordinary child of his age.

Fliss watched, rather jealous of the way Matt had taken to this big stranger. Was there nothing Nick Da Costa wasn't prepared to interfere with?

'Hallo, Fliss—you found them, then.' Mrs Meredith, youthful in her Jaeger dress, approached without anyone noticing.

'Hallo, Mum!' Fliss kissed her on the cheek. 'I hear you've had a personal tour of the Paediatric Unit.' She tried to sound less antagonistic than she felt. 'Kate took you, did she?'

'Yes, we met her while we were waiting for you in Reception. I asked how Melanie Higgins, one of the referrals from the Infirmary, was doing and Kate offered to show me round.' Kate had been for a weekend at Fliss's home once and had got on like a house on fire with

Dr Meredith, whose views were quietly feminist. 'There are a couple of very interesting cases up there. I don't suppose you get to see kids much, though, do you? Matt!'

Matt, bored by the conversation, had attempted to climb back on to the bulldozer and Nick had gone to supervise, offering a helping hand—just as Matt's large foot in its sturdy Kicker shot out. Nick, caught in the vitals and worse, gave an agonised whoosh of breath and almost doubled up.

'Mr Da Costa—I'm *so* sorry! Matt, come down from there.' Fliss stood back while her mother eased the surgeon upright and offered advice on how to cope with winding.

'Well done,' murmured Fliss sotto voce to her little brother, who had hardly noticed what had happened. That should keep Highstead's resident sex symbol out of action for an hour or two!

'I'd ask you to come with us for lunch,' Dr Meredith was saying as they approached, 'but we normally only go to McDonald's or something like that. It's easier, you see.' She looked fleetingly in Matt's direction, as if to explain that her son couldn't be bothered to sit still in a restaurant for an hour while a proper meal was served.

'I'm busy, anyway,' Nick apologised. 'But I would certainly like to talk some more on the . . .' He saw Fliss's sharp eyes watching, the tight line of her mouth as she guessed what he had cooked up. 'On the—er— subject,' he finished ambiguously.

'Perhaps you could come to tea this evening, at Fliss's place. It's not far up the hill,' Dr Meredith suggested. 'I'm sure she wouldn't mind.'

'I look forward to it. See you later, Matt.' With a brief

wave that included them all, Nick was off, back into the main building.

'I do mind, actually. I mind very much indeed.' Fliss was sitting on a bench at St Katharine's Dock, a melting ice-cream cone in one hand. 'He's been very critical—of me, of Dad . . . I really don't think you ought to get involved in his schemes; think of what Dad will say when he finds out that one of his detractors will be operating on his son!'

'I don't think he'd mind as much as you seem to think,' Dr Meredith smiled enigmatically. 'He's got nothing but good to say for Mr Da Costa as far as I remember. Anyway, it's all a formality at the moment—and I haven't even expressed my interest in the idea yet. A lot will depend on Matt and whether his heart's up to it.'

Fliss watched her brother dancing on the deck of one of the boats moored for tourists to clamber over—steam ships and Norfolk wherries and fishing smacks, all in their original condition—and said lightly, 'Oh, I don't think there's anything wrong with his heart!'

'And Dr Thomas didn't, either,' her mother laughed.

'What do you know about Nick Da Costa?' asked Fliss carefully, lest her interest be misconstrued.

'Not much,' her mother shaded her eyes to keep watch over Matt. 'Don't go too near the edge, darling! Your father mentioned him once or twice in telephone calls— seemed rather impressed, I think. He was sad to have to leave him holding the reins when the project dropped through, I know. I think probably Dad felt that you'd be interested in the work he was doing over there . . . Matt, come and have your ice-cream before it disappears completely!'

Fliss felt a lump rise in her throat. Had her father mentioned her to Nick when they'd met? Had he gone on in his typically bullish fashion about his bright young daughter and her interest in a career in plastic and cosmetic and reconstructive surgery? She cringed. Her father, like most fathers, tended to think his children were the best thing since sliced bread. No wonder Nick had had it in for her if he'd had the Sir Mortimer version of her talents and ambitions! To hide her sudden confusion, she called to Matt and took him off to board the bright red lightship, its beacon in a huge glass dome, docked alongside a wonderfully old-fashioned steam packet. On their way to the river, Matt excitedly sitting in the front seat on top of a double-decker bus, Sheila Meredith had talked seriously to her daughter about having minor surgery done to aid Matt's appearance.

'I think you're making a lot of fuss about nothing,' she told Fliss, unable to understand her daughter's strong reaction against the idea. 'Just think; if his tongue is sorted out he won't be bothered so much by it; and he won't get a sore mouth, either. And if it means he can lead a more normal life and people don't shun him in the street it'll be all to his benefit. *His* benefit, Fliss. Not yours or mine, because we accept him as he is.'

Fliss had rumbled on, unwilling to admit that it was a good idea. But the more rationally she considered it, the less objection there appeared to be. It was just the way Nick Da Costa and Kate had bludgeoned them into it . . .

The afternoon passed pleasantly; the sun shone on them as they took a boat from the pier at the Tower of London, a brief walk from St Katharine's Dock with its lovely river frontage and converted warehouses, down to Westminster, pointing out all the landmarks on the way to an enthralled Matt. He was disappointed that Tower Bridge wouldn't open for them and most amused by the Guardsmen in their bearskins. The mock-Gothic architecture of the Houses of Parliament failed to impress, but the striking of Big Ben did. He got a little flustered when he had to jump on to an escalator to go home on the Tube, but the ride itself—how *did* the doors close all on their own?—more than made up for it.

They arrived back at Fliss's flat shortly before five—and found Nick Da Costa sitting on the front wall, his legs swinging nonchalantly as he waited for them. Fliss's heart leapt at the mere sight of him.

'Did you have a good time?' he asked Matt, who went tearing up to him to give him a hug. And again that pang of hurt twisted in her.

Such a wonderful time had he had that Matt was almost incoherent in his recounting of the afternoon's entertainments. And equally incoherent with joy when he saw Fliss's present—a tough trail bicycle that he could ride round the local fields or up to Jill's place when he went to ride his pony.

'Will he be able to manage it?' Nick looked dubiously at the bike and then at Matt, who was sitting on the floor by it and idly turning the pedals with his hands.

'Of course he can,' snapped Fliss. 'Being a bit simple doesn't affect his sense of balance!'

Nick said nothing. He took in Fliss's tall, straight body in incongruous casuals. Even like this there was an air of no-nonsense about her, something which he found immensely appealing and amusing. But her strained mouth and pale complexion told him that now was not the time to argue or ask questions.

Fliss, aware that she was behaving badly—and, what was more, suspiciously—went off to the kitchen to get some tea, and before long they sat down to a riotous meal guaranteed to satisfy adults and Matt alike. There was cold salmon she had slaved over the night before, with salad and crusty bread for those who liked it; and sandwiches and crisps and sausages on sticks for those who liked their party fare a little more traditional. Fliss had dug out some old Christmas crackers that Matt was always fond of and they had candles on the table, even though it was still early and the sun shone in brightly.

And when they had eaten what they wanted of that, she brought in her pièce de résistance; the cake.

'What is it, dear?' Mrs Meredith was brave enough to ask.

'It's a pony!' Fliss tried to sound hurt, but was too amused by the thing on the cake board to succeed. She'd tried to create a Thelwell pony, trimming the cake to size, resting it on short legs, giving it a carefully sculpted mane and tail and saddle.

'Now you tell me . . . yes, I suppose it does look like a pony,' the guests grudgingly agreed.

'Well, it's chocolate. And if you don't fancy that, I've made a summer pudding and we can have it with cream.' The question was addressed to Nick, for Fliss knew well enough that her mother would opt for pudding and Matt for cake.

'You know how much I love chocolate,' he laughed. 'I'll take the horse.' Fliss gingerly sliced a piece from her creation's rump and placed it in front of him, repeating the process for Matt, who set to eagerly and was soon covered in chocolate butter cream.

'It's delicious—it's absolutely wonderful! How clever you are, Mrs Meredith, to have brought up a daughter who can do a neat cholecystectomy *and* cook.'

'How do you look after yourself at the moment?' Mrs Meredith, ignoring the secret communication that seemed to be going on between the two surgeons, a language of meaningful glances and sharp retorts, determined to make Nick feel welcome.

'I'm renting a flat. It's some way away. I eat at the hospital mainly,' he said, helping himself to more cake.

'And you eat out in expensive restaurants most evenings, don't forget,' Fliss said coolly.

'I'm getting to know the locals,' he agreed smoothly. 'It's an important part of settling into a new area, isn't it? Very often, of course, the people one meets and encourages at first are dropped later.'

His devilishly dark eyes challenged her provocatively. What did he mean? Fliss felt a chill sweep over her. Was he implying that though they'd got to know each other fairly quickly—disastrously quickly, perhaps—he didn't expect the acquaintance to last?

'I'll go and start the washing-up,' she said quickly. 'Matt, into the bathroom and wash your face this instant—and don't touch anything until you're clean!'

'We'll take Matt up to the Heath for half an hour to practise on his new bike,' said Nick firmly, 'and give you a few minutes on your own. You've had a long day, you need to relax for a while.' He came into the kitchen, leaning casually on the door post. 'Would it be all right by you if we were to take Matt's bike with us on Sunday and drop it off on the way home so that your mother doesn't have to struggle home with it on the train?'

'I hadn't thought of that.' Fliss ran a soapy hand through her hair before she realised what she was doing. 'If it's no inconvenience to you . . .'

'None at all,' he said simply, and turned away to lead the rest of the family up the road and on to the wide open spaces of the Heath where Matt could fall off his bike to his heart's content and he and Mrs Meredith could talk in more detail about admitting Matt for minor surgery.

Nick refused to let himself think about Fliss or her erratic behaviour. Some people were like that about family; was she embarrassed that he should have seen her brother? He couldn't believe that. She made him so angry sometimes—he just wanted to kiss her and make her quiet.

An hour later and Matt and his mum were on their way in the taxi that Fliss had ordered for them. As she waved them off, Fliss's heart beat heavily in her breast. For Nick Da Costa stood menacingly at the side of the road with her, and from the occasional dark glances that had come her way she knew that trouble lay ahead.

'Well, it was nice of you to come,' she said boldly on the pavement, doing her best to deter him from re-entering the house. 'I expect you've got things to do now.'

'I've got plenty of time, as it happens,' he said grimly, and without so much as a by-your-leave, took Fliss firmly by the arm and led her back to her flat.

'Why didn't you tell me?' he growled as soon as the door was safely shut on them and Fliss was trapped with him in her own home. His eyes were like black coals, sparkling with annoyance, as he thrust her on to the sofa and stood over her.

'Tell you what?' she said defiantly, sitting up straight and shaking out a cushion as if he wasn't really there.

'About Matt and everything else. Can you imagine how I felt when Kate introduced us?' He thrust his hands into his pockets and fixed her with an inescapable stare. 'Well? Are you going to explain?'

'Explain what?' she said belligerently. 'You're in my house without my invitation; you've just had a meal with my family without my invitation; and you've just coerced my mother into having unnecessary surgery performed on my brother—and you have the damned nerve to stand there demanding that *I* explain?' Her firm chin jutting defiantly, Fliss resolved to stare him out.

'Why didn't you tell me about Matt when we were having that . . . that discussion about Down's kids?' he began again. 'You provoked me into saying all kinds of unjust things!'

'Because I was waiting for an opportunity like this to let you know,' Fliss managed from between gritted teeth. 'You think you know everything, don't you?' She tossed back her soft brown hair and gave a rough imitation of the way he'd spoken to her that afternoon on the children's ward. '*When you know something about Down's children*—that was it, I seem to remember. Not the slightest willingness to believe that I could have feelings about anything within my experience. Spoilt little Fliss Meredith, I can see you thinking it—not just thinking it; you damn well as nearly told my boss that he'd only employed me because my father is famous!'

She paused, eyes blazing, short of breath. Nick, thoroughly taken aback by such an onslaught, took his hands out of his pockets and eased himself into the chair opposite her, sitting carefully on the edge, as if to pounce if she went too far.

'Why didn't you ask me? Why didn't you ask if I'd had any experience of these children?' she asked more softly, the edge of her anger abated now. 'You always want to think the worst of me, and I don't understand why. My father respects you!' Her wide eyes pleaded eloquently for some understanding.

'Your father again! He's got nothing to do with it,' spluttered Nick. 'The fact is that I can help your brother and your mother and you're being obstructive! I don't understand you, Fliss. Sometimes we seem to get on well—and then this afternoon you're practically rude to me every time you open your mouth . . . It shouldn't be like this,' he said more gently. 'We should at least be able to be more reasonable.'

'How can I be reasonable when you've ruined my life? I had things all neatly planned before you came along. Since you've been at Highstead you've done nothing but make a fool of me. I was doing what I wanted, I was happy—I loved my work . . .' Fliss buried her face in her hands, trying to control all the anger and frustration that was threatening to emerge as tears; tears were a sign of weakness and weakness would only make him more scathing of her. She would *not* allow him more ammunition with which he could destroy her.

Nick watched, stunned, as his words came back to him; part of him felt angry with her for leading him on over this Matt affair, making him appear a fool, but a larger part recognised that he had been too tough.

'Oh, Fliss . . .' He knelt beside her and put an arm round her shoulders, and suddenly she wanted nothing more than to bury her face against his chest, to cling to him and have him enfold her in safety and warmth and security. But she held back. It would be the biggest mistake of her life.

'Go away. You've ruined my life,' she muttered gruffly, her voice betraying something of how she felt.

'No, I haven't. Your life is only just beginning,' Nick murmured gently, pulling her into him so that she seemed to fuse with him. All his pretence was forgotten now; all his stupid schemes to bring this coldhearted young schemer to her knees. Because in a way, even though it was him who knelt with her in his arms, he had succeeded; he had broken down the barriers, the barriers that had only existed in his imagination and her inexperience. And behind them he found a desirable young woman, warm and tender in his hands.

'Look at me,' he whispered. Fliss raised her head, caught in the spell of the moment, caution and canniness swept away by her misery and tiredness. 'There are no illusions now,' he said, stroking her hair from her brow as if she was a child. 'I know who you are, what you're like, and I promise I won't jump the gun again.'

Her eyes were like pools of brown fire as his mouth lowered gently to hers, his lips explored her own. For a second Fliss resisted, holding back from him, feeling the warmth and fervour of his kisses but refusing to respond. And then suddenly the gulf opened before her and she could no longer prevent herself from falling into its dark heart. Hungry for him, she parted her lips, held him to her, ran her fingers through his unruly hair while he teased her with consummate skill, seeming to find the very core of her with his seeking lips and those black, black eyes. She gave a little sob of surrender and her last vestiges of resistance fell from her. The tension and fury of the day faded to oblivion. All that mattered was Nick, the man who had destroyed her ordered existence but had opened the door to something new—something infinitely more dangerous than a quiet life as a dedicated surgeon, but something with rewards incalculable.

Nick pulled away for a second and took her with him, laying her gently on the old Persian rug in front of the fireplace. He seemed to sway above her as he ran a hand lightly over her flat stomach in the thin trousers, circling it slowly upwards until it fleetingly brushed the tip of one breast, then the other. Fliss, in exquisite torment, reached up to pull him down to her, to cover her, but he held back, a smile crossing his enigmatic face.

'Do you still want that job on the unit?' he asked teasingly, his hands caressing her still fully-clothed body until she purred beneath them.

'What?' she murmured in a voice cracked with emotion.

'It's yours for the asking,' he smiled, at last relinquishing and settling by her side, his mouth on hers again, the hardness of his body pressed to her.

A spark of intelligence seemed to flow like a patent fire extinguisher through her body, dousing the flames that licked her from head to toe and filling her with an icy realisation of just what was happening. Nick was bribing her; if she gave herself to him now, her job on the team was guaranteed. And if she didn't?

She struggled to free herself from his embrace, but he restrained her; suddenly she was aware of his strength, the cast-iron muscles of that carefully conditioned body that had so traitorously set her heart thudding for him. They had set off this physical response and they could force her to something she now definitely didn't want.

'Let me go!' Nick, stunned, released her instantly, his mind racing, his body urging him to proceed. A sharp pain of something new to him, something that he had only experienced in the last week or so, overtook him. He just wanted to cradle Fliss in his arms if that was all *she* wanted. He was content just to be with her; he would never force her.

'Get out! Go on. Unlike some of your other *friends*, I don't sleep with men for promotion,' snapped Fliss, pushing him further away, lest those dark eyes tempt her again with their sensual promise. 'Directors use casting couches—I'm surprised you haven't stooped so low as to invite ambitious young women to display their talents on your examination couch, Mr Da Costa!'

'I don't have one—not yet, anyway. My surgery hasn't been built yet,' he replied with ice in his tone. 'Would you prefer to audition there in six weeks' time? For God's sake, Fliss, I thought you'd be pleased that I'd decided to offer you the job!'

'It's still on offer, is it?' she asked furiously, pulling down her T-shirt that seemed to have been well on the way up to her neck.

'Of course. Calm down . . .' He reached out and stroked her arm enticingly.

'Out! I told you, I'm not paying for the privilege of working with you except by my legitimate labour. You're jumping to irrational conclusions again.' She scrambled to her feet, her hands and knees shaking as she realised just how close she had come to letting him triumph over her.

'You're still a child,' mumbled Nick as he climbed to his feet and reached for his discarded jacket and tie. 'I just want to show you how to grow up. But obviously I'm not required.'

With a glance that seemed to penetrate to her very soul and set it reeling, he opened the door and walked out into the dark hall. Moonlight sparkled through the glass in the front door and set his eyes blazing with brilliant white light.

'The job offer is there if you want it, Fliss. But I wonder if you dare accept the challenge. Because it's not like general surgery where you whip something out or repair with a stitch; it's hard emotional and physical grind, sometimes for years and sometimes heartbreaking, and it needs an inner strength for a surgeon to cope with it. You're damned good at what you're doing at the moment and you're fine with the patients. But I wonder if there's something lacking inside . . . Something that won't grow up, won't admit that it's there?'

He waited, and all she could hear was his steady breathing and the tick of her grandmother's clock on the mantelpiece.

'Let me know when you decide what to do. Maybe I can help.'

And then there was just the slam of the door and his footsteps echoing down the path.

CHAPTER EIGHT

'OF course, you know what everyone will think. There's no smoke without fire—I reckon that's the hospital gossipmonger's favourite phrase.' Kate lay in the garden of Fliss's house on a big plaid rug spread on the roughly cropped grass and reached for her glass of lemon laced ever so slightly with gin and soda water and clinking with ice cubes.

Fliss sat miserably at her side in a skimpy vest top, trying to enjoying soaking up the sun—but her whirring mind wouldn't let her. Two days she had had to contemplate Nick Da Costa's parting shot. Two days in which to anatomise her life and her personality—and still she had no answer.

'But I reckon you should take it, all the same,' Kate rambled on, her brain fuddled by that heat. 'It's what you've wanted all along, isn't it? So who cares what people'll say? It won't be long before you're able to prove to them that you're there for your surgical skill alone, not favours rendered under the sheets.'

'You're absolutely sure that he's offered that staff nurse on the children's ward a job on the Seymour?' Fliss asked for the third time, as if she hadn't quite absorbed it.

'Yes. She does have relevant experience, I'll admit,' Kate said grudgingly. 'She worked at the burns unit in Bangor.'

'Well then! It doesn't necessarily mean that he's only recruiting his ex-girl-friends, does it?' muttered Fliss indignantly. 'You'll be telling me he's taking Jane on as a Sister next!'

'How is she? Shall we invite her down for a drink?' Kate glanced up at the closed windows of the top floor. 'I don't think she's in. Pity.'

Fliss didn't feel the same regret; not because Jane had done anything to jeopardise the relationship but simply because of her relationship with Nick Da Costa. 'She's not around much these days,' she said absently, rather relieved at Kate's admission that sexual conquest was not the only criterion by which he was choosing the unit staff.

They both lay back contentedly in the sun, Kate's bleeper at her elbow and the sitting-room window wide open should the telephone ring—because they were both on duty. Fliss had managed to swop her Sunday stint for Friday and had so far had an easy time of it, with an unbroken night last night, but it was unlikely to go on being so quiet.

She had decided at last to confide in Kate. Not everything—not by a very long chalk. It was enough to admit that Nick Da Costa had changed his mind but that he seemed to expect certain rather intimate favours in exchange for the position.

'I expect he's only concerned in getting to know you properly before you start working together on the team,' Kate yawned now, easing her bikini top as low as she dared without exciting the attention of the middle-aged man who lived next door and kept peering nonchalantly over the fence at them as he did his gardening. 'After all, it's a matter of temperament as much as anything, isn't it? You ought to be jolly grateful to Barney for chucking himself down those steps, you know, otherwise you'd never have got the chance to work with Nick and he'd never have spotted your potential. How is Barney, by the way?'

'I called him and he's getting better. He's had to have another op to sort out a cartilage problem, but he should be home on crutches before long.' Fliss laughed. 'All those children! They'll trip him up every way he turns!'

Kate giggled. 'Any more of this stuff?' She held up her empty glass.

'Go and make it yourself. You owe me a few favours after waylaying Mum and Matt the other day.'

'I've told you what happened,' Kate got lazily to her feet. 'Another glass of this mixture and that will be my final apology—not that I'm really apologetic about it at all. It's for Matt's own good, you know,' she grumbled as she made the trek through Peter's back door and up through the house to Fliss's kitchen.

'Your friend left you? How'd you like some company?' The pinkly balding head of Mr Howard from next door popped up immediately Kate departed. He rested arms sunburned and encased from the elbow up in a Hawaiian print shirt on the top of the fence and smiled ingratiatingly at her. 'You work at the hospital, don't you?' he went on. 'Are you nurses or secretaries or what?'

'Oh, go away!' Fliss made a rude gesture and rolled over on to her stomach. All she needed now were the attentions of an amorous neighbour.

Kate came back only seconds later, having discovered all the necessary ingredients for her concoction in Peter's flat.

'Oh, don't mind her,' she said cheerfully, putting down the tray on the rug. 'She's a brilliant brain surgeon and she's been up all night working on the latest transplant.'

'Ah!' With a look that said that he'd obviously met a couple of complete maniacs, Mr Howard gaily waved goodbye and retreated to his own side of the fence.

'You're very smart. Wouldn't you feel more comfortable in something a bit lighter? I'll put Matt's bike in the boot of the car while you change.' Nick Da Costa stood in the hallway looking quite impossibly delectable in faded blue jeans and a collarless white shirt, crisply ironed; a far contrast to Fliss's smart coffee-striped dress and matching jacket.

'I thought that as it was an official visit—' she tried to explain.

'You'll spend most of the day in a theatre gown,' Nick said reasonably. 'You might at least ensure that you're comfortable for the drive.'

Without further ado a subdued Fliss shrugged and went into her bedroom. Jeans, she decided, would be too casual. But she did rummage around and find a full Tana lawn skirt in muted shades of green and blue and pink, with a matching short-sleeved blouse. She put them on hurriedly and decided she would have done far better to choose the outfit first thing that morning. Running a brush through her hair, she sped out to the car where Nick was waiting.

He waited for her to do up her seat-belt. 'What happened to that chap who went through the windscreen?' he asked quietly, breaking the uncomfortable silence. 'I wasn't able to follow him up.'

'He was transferred to Mr Amery's firm,' said Fliss, fascinated by Nick's brown hand confidently manipulating the gear-stick as they moved off. There was such strength in even the smallest, most elegant moves he made. 'I've just popped over to see him once or twice and he's doing very well. The nose is absolutely perfect, though I say so myself.'

There was another pause as they climbed the hill and continued northwards, heading for the North Circular. 'I saw Mrs Nicholls yesterday afternoon,' Fliss blurted to fill the silence. 'She's very cheerful and the drain's coming out today. You don't mind, do you?'

'I told you, I'm busy—the follow-ups are yours. If you say the drain is ready to come out, I believe you. Okay?'

He turned to look meaningly at her and a smile broke his so far impassive face. 'Are you all right? I did some pretty straight talking the other night.'

'You certainly did,' she agreed dispassionately.

'And?' He glanced at her again, taking in her pensive expression and the shadows under her eyes that told him she hadn't slept very well lately.

'Let's see how today goes first,' she said, watching the passing grey landscape intently. Already the simple fact of being near him was working its spell. Already her mind was filled with all sorts of delicious fancies, images of him naked, tender . . . 'Tell me what we're going to do today,' she said to distract her train of thought.

'We're going up to a research clinic attached to the Oxford medical school—though for some reason it's in Birmingham. Brian Heyward, who taught me much of what I learned in this country before I went to the States, has a young patient there whose skull was badly shattered in an industrial accident. He shouldn't really have survived, but he did, and now he's got a lopsided face because much of the bone around the temple and eye had to be removed after the accident. To make him look a bit prettier and give him the psychological boost he needs, we're going to take chips from his pelvis and hip joint and shape them to fit the existing bone structure.'

Nick waited, as if for questions.

'The bone will take and knit, I presume?' she asked casually. It was a skilled operation and hardly a common one, but she knew the medical theory behind it.

'Yes. We peel the facial skin from a forward cranial incision, which will be covered by the hairline. He'll look a little odd at first, but give it a couple of months and he'll be happy to go out on the streets.' Nick watched Fliss's hands relaxed in her lap, pleased that she wasn't on tenterhooks, eager to impress when out with him. Not like some women who insisted on talking all the time in an effort to persuade him how entertaining they were.

'Can I put a cassette on?' she asked, and wondered why he smiled so warmly as he showed her where they were kept. Dear Fliss, he thought as he turned up the M40. Dear down-to-earth Fliss; no chatter, no recriminations about the other evening, no flutter about where they were going and what were they going to do and would she be all right; just gentle acceptance and a quiet confidence that everything would be fine. He relaxed for the first time in forty-eight hours, forgetting the pendulum swing of recriminations, the realisation of his insensitivity, his anger with her. How nice it would be to have such a passenger by his side always . . . The bachelor voice of freedom shrieked a warning in his skull; this way lay roots and responsibilities, it cried. This would spell the end of his adventures, his pleasures. But just at the moment Nick felt inclined to ignore the warning.

'Ah, Nick's protégée! Glad you could come, Miss Meredith.' Brian Heyward was a sandy-haired man in his early fifties with a lank strand of hair coiled carefully over his bald patch and a toothy grin that more than made up for his lack of physical magnetism.

'Nick! Here you are again, lad! Are you up to your eyes in cement down there at Highstead? You're very lucky to have got that, you know. There are still one or two people around who can teach you a thing or two,' he laughed heartily.

'Show them to me,' Nick growled mockingly to Fliss while his old mentor went on effusively.

'Would you like coffee, Miss Meredith?' He gestured expansively in the direction of a coffee machine.

'Fliss,' she grinned. 'No, we had coffee and food on the way up. We thought you'd want to get started immediately.'

'Marvellous, marvellous. Let's go and see our man, then, shall we? He's had a pre-med, so he shouldn't mind a mass visit.' He ushered them out of the reception room and off to the small ward where the select few patients chosen for treatment were billeted in comfort unparalleled at Highstead. 'Done anything interesting recently?' he was asking Nick as they all strode down the corridor. Out of the corner of her eye Fliss saw Nick's mouth twitch, though his head was bowed in apparent thought as Brian quizzed him about a technical problem they'd been having. Nick looked up suddenly, caught Fliss's gaze and gave her a wink that said, 'Sorry about this—but you know what it's like when you meet an old teacher . . .'

'Good man, Nick. You're very lucky to be working under him,' said Brian as he and Fliss stood together in the small scrub room next to the operating theatre. Nick was already prepared and demanding his favourite MacEwan's chisel and specialised rugines.

'I'm flattered,' Fliss murmured noncommittally, trying to ensure that the new-fangled disposable paper dungaree-styled coveralls she had been issued with weren't revealing more of her person than intended. They were huge on her. To be told all this, having already been introduced as Nick's protégée . . . She felt amused and bemused.

'He's tough—but I dare say you've discovered that,' Brian flapped about in ungainly fashion, even funnier now in his mob-cap and gown. 'But fair, and such a good surgeon. I was sorry to see him go, but he had to move to the States—more money over there, you see, better facilities. He was a bit wild as a student,' the older man said reminiscently. 'One for the ladies, I remember . . .'

'He still is,' laughed Fliss. 'Highstead's nurses are unanimous in their presentation of hearts on platters!'

'Not nearly as wild as he was.' Brian looked surprised. 'He used to disappear for days on end as a student. I think he went through one of those crises, whether he wanted to be a doctor or not. It would have been a great waste if he hadn't—don't you agree?' he asked.

'Oh yes, a great loss,' Fliss smiled a little.

'I've been hearing all about your student days,' she whispered over the operating table as they assembled to begin the operating list. 'You wicked young thing— what happened in the meantime? Where's the mean, moody, deeply sensitive creature you once were?' she laughed.

'I told you,' Nick raised one sexy eyebrow over the mask in a laconic gesture that made Fliss's heart expand with pleasure, 'we all have to grow up. I did and so has your friend Peter—he grew up and got out. Your turn to decide what to do now.'

Before Fliss could reply, Brian Heyward and his surgeon entered and discussion about the operation began. Fliss was to work with Brian on preparing the

patient's smashed temple and cheekbone for the implant
of bone that Nick and the other man were going to chip
from the iliac fossa.

The actual chipping away of suitable bone fragments
was a tough, strenuous job, and Fliss and Brian stood
back from the table as Nick used orthopaedic hammers
and chisels to complete the task.

'This area is almost always the most useful,' Nick
showed Fliss the crown of the pelvic joint. It was a grisly
sight, but one which she knew would soon regenerate.

'Which will be the most painful in the immediate
post-operative period?' she asked quietly.

'Oh, the hip, very definitely,' Brian answered at her
side. 'In fact we try to keep the patients sedated fairly
heavily for the first few days. With two such diverse and
major traumas it helps recovery considerably.'

Before long, Nick had enough bone fragments to
please him and Brian Heywood's young assistant, a
German, moved in to repair the donor site and stitch up.
The attentions of the team travelled up the patient's
body to the new site. Using fine calipers to judge the size
of implant required, Nick carved the donor bone into
jigsaw pieces, kept artificially cool and moist to preserve
their life—for bone, like any other tissue, could die—
and Fliss and Brian held them in position with fine-
toothed forceps.

'We're very lucky, working on this area,' Nick commented as he worked. 'There's fortunately not a great
deal of blood—that's sometimes a problem. How's the
anaesthetic?'

The anaesthetist, working intravenously, for the
proximity of the operation site to the nose and mouth,
through which gas was normally administered, meant
that the most common method of narcosis was out of the

question, gave a thumbs-up sign. 'Not long now,' said
Brian after a glance at the clock.

Fliss followed his gaze and discovered that they had
been working for almost three hours, right through
lunch—which was presumably why Nick had insisted
that they halt on the way to Birmingham and have
something to eat. She could still scarcely believe that she
was here, or that this complex and fascinating operation
was going on in front of her very eyes.

'Now Fliss comes into her own.' Nick, having assured
himself that the jigsaw of bone pieces was all correctly
positioned and impairing nothing, motioned her to come
over. 'Finish off, will you? Your stitching and feel for
skin is better than mine.'

Under her mask, Fliss blushed, noticing how Brian
looked on in fascination from his old pupil to his pupil's
pupil. But, knowing that she was quite capable of doing
what was asked of her, she took over while the other
three watched. It was not a simple matter of stitching;
the various subcutaneous layers, some with scar tissue
from the original injury and earlier surgery, had to be
matched and excised. What remained had to be eased
over the new bone structure, matched with the patient's
undamaged side . . . Fliss took her time, pulling gently,
trying not to get the characteristic tight look that women
who had had face-lifts and ear-tucks suffered if their
surgeon was having a busy day.

At nearly four o'clock she put the last stitch in and
stood back to look at her handiwork. For the past hour
she had thought of nothing but what she was doing, the
job in hand; now her back ached and her feet were
sweaty in her rubber boots, provided by this go-ahead
clinic.

'How's that?' Nick and Brian had wandered off halfway through the process to discuss what had been done. Now they came back and inspected the neat lines of stitching.

'Excellent.' Brian, in newly sterile gloves, bent closer to make his examination. 'Give him six weeks and he won't know he was ever in trouble,' he smiled.

Fliss helped the Theatre Sister to dress the wounds and thanked her for her help and patience before the patient disappeared through the swing doors and into the recovery room before going up for a few days' intensive care. Tired and drained though she felt, she also had a singing sensation in her veins that, should she care to jump off a high building, she would be able to fly!

Still later she sat in Brian's office enjoying a refreshing cup of tea and participating in a useful discussion of what they'd done and hadn't done; what was particular to this patient and what variations they might expect to find. In these clinical surroundings—for the place was very modern indeed, quite unlike Highstead's hybrid development—it was so easy to forget Nick's impact as a man and just concentrate on him as an exceptionally capable surgeon. It had always been true for Fliss that the magic of the theatre and the need to concentrate had allowed her to escape her everyday worries; with the lights and muffled silence creating a cocoon from the world, surrounded by stainless steel and swathed bodies and with all the technical language bandied about, it was like being in a time capsule. In theatre you didn't know if it was raining or snowing outside; whether governments had fallen or friends were being unfaithful. Sometimes it was a blessing—and sometimes a curse that divorced surgeons from the real world.

Before they said goodbye, Nick and Fliss donned gowns and masks and entered the sterile area of

Intensive Care to see their patient for the last time. Fliss looked admiringly around the small tiled rooms with their shiny floors and internal monitoring systems so that nurses didn't have to waste time sitting at bedsides.

'I take it the new unit will be something like this,' Fliss said with interest.

'Something like this, yes, though things have changed even since this place was built,' Nick responded non-committally. 'Don't you like it?'

'Well, it's a bit impersonal . . .'

'My God! I suppose you want carpet on the floor and hideous flowered bed curtains like those in Men's Medical!' he exploded. 'I know the mystique of medicine is getting very technical and that ordinary people find it a bit daunting—but the whole point of a place like this is that it's clean and allows us to do things that have never been done before . . .'

'It's all right,' laughed Fliss, drawing him from the ward, suddenly conscious that she had put her hand on to his arm and could feel its warmth and muscular solidity under her fingers like a warm shock; like putting your fingers on the sole of a heating iron and knowing it's only going to get hotter—and daring yourself to keep them there until you get burnt. And get burnt was exactly what would happen, she warned herself, dropping his arm as if it had just reached that crucial, unbearable heat.

But it was too late; the spell of professionalism had been shattered. Reaching round behind her to undo her neck-tie that was holding the pale blue sterile gown in place, Nick forced her back against the wall of the corridor. No one was around; since it was a specialised unit with patients from all over the country, there were few visitors, and its modern conveniences had done away with the bustling nurses who haunted every corner of Highstead.

'We have some unfinished business.' Instead of feeling the warmth of just his arm, Fliss was aware of the fire of his entire body as he pressed her firmly into the unyielding wall. His thighs were pinned against hers, his chest rubbed her breasts; he leaned his elbows against the wall at either side of her head. She was forced to look deep into his dancing black eyes—and to experience the deepseated thrill of raw sexuality that flared within her.

'Did you enjoy the operation?' he asked in a strangely deep voice. But Fliss could tell, with every muscle of her body, that he had his mind elsewhere.

'Yes,' she muttered dryly, pushing gently against him and only succeeding in proving to her own satisfaction that the very same feelings of desire were coursing through him, too. 'Someone will come,' she protested, having to force the words from her throat.

'A kiss and I'll let you go. You're my protégée now, remember; my professional partner—and what's kiss between workmates?'

Fliss hesitated for a moment, her eyes absorbing his slight growth of dark beard, the freshly showered scent of his skin, the full curve of a lip that looked as if it had been subtly defined in white pencil. Almost involuntarily her lips parted—and Nick took his cue and kissed her deeply, burying himself in the sweetness of her mouth and cradling her head to him as if he somehow imagined that the emotional explosions he was experiencing inside himself might blow it off.

Fliss could scarcely breathe and didn't care as she kissed him back, returning his bruising pressure with candid fervour—and then dimly she heard a familiar noise, the thrum of a trolley approaching down a tiled corridor. She pulled back. Nick, startled, only clutched her to him tighter, but the look in her eye made him listen and they drew apart just as another comatose patient arrived for intensive care.

'Thank goodness that, for all the miracles of modern science, they still haven't invented a silent theatre trolley,' she laughed gently, watching Nick's smile of recognition as they headed back to Brian's office for the last time.

'They're here!' Matt's shout greeted them from behind the garden gate, then suddenly it opened and he raced out to greet them. 'Where's my bike?' he yelled, and promptly ran to the back of the car where Nick was already easing it out.

'Steady on,' he grumbled as Matt tugged, 'I don't want you to go chipping my paintwork. Here it is!'

Matt had already forgotten their presence as he climbed on to the saddle and pushed precariously off. Whatever his handicaps, physical courage wasn't among them, and he was soon pedalling down the garden path and round the mellow stone house whose old gabled windows winked in the slowly setting sun. Birdsong rang across the still Sunday sky and the scent of a bonfire was just beginning to touch the air.

'Come in and have some supper,' Fliss invited Nick. 'At least come in and say hallo to Mum. The two of you are old plotters, remember.'

'I wouldn't dream of driving off without making myself known to your wonderful mother,' laughed Nick. Since they had left the clinic he had been relaxed, warm in her company, as if another barrier had been broken, and now he followed her through the front garden, full of old cottage roses and spreading, old-fashioned herbaceous plants, and round to the back door. A delicious smell of hot jam reached them—but it was not Mrs Meredith who greeted them.

In his well-worn gardening togs—tattered flared trousers from an earlier era and a psychedelically printed shirt with the sleeves buttoned to protect his arms from the thorns of his beloved roses—Sir Mortimer Meredith did not look quite the dragon Nick remembered. But despite that fact, and the realisation that the great man was in his bare feet and, good lord, actually had bunions! Nick's hackles rose.

'Dad! Matt didn't tell us that you were here!' Sir Mortimer turned to acknowledge his visitors properly and his luminous brown eyes glowed piercingly from behind his bank-clerkish horn-rimmed spectacles. Nick stood back for a moment as father and daughter, much of a muchness in height, embraced. Fliss didn't seem to see anything amiss in her father's garish attire; Nick cringed at the very idea of going near such a shirt.

Suddenly he was brought up short with the visual proof of the fact of Fliss's background. Her mother he thought charming. Her father . . .

'Mr Da Costa, how pleasant to see you.' Sir Mortimer's shrewd eyes had taken in everything, particularly Nick's frozen look of polite uninterest. 'I'm so very sorry that we had to part last time on such acrimonious grounds. I do hope that your new position at Highstead suits you—though I still regret very much not being able to work with you. Mr Da Costa's pioneering work in reconstructive surgery is second to none;' he explained to his daughter, though he knew darn well that Da Costa and Fliss were old acquaintances.

Faced with such charm, Nick was forced to put on his best smile and murmur some pleasantry about how good it was to see Sir Mortimer again. Fliss watched him, an encouraging smile on her face and her insides performing amazing contortions. Please don't let them start wrangling, she thought desperately. All the old tensions that had been dissolved during the day began to make themselves felt again. She simply couldn't bear it if Nick started playing the 'me or your father' game with her.

'I don't normally greet guests in such attire,' Sir Mortimer apologised airily, 'but I've been hacking away at the undergrowth at the end of the garden. It's so good to wield a machete occasionally, instead of working down a microscope. But this is *too* awful,' he said, pulling at the vile shirt.

'Oh, I agree,' said Nick with cool ambiguity. Fliss moved to his side and gave him a firm nudge in the ribs—but before true warfare could break out, Mrs Meredith arrived and immediately packed her compliant husband off upstairs for a shower.

'I'll make a light supper,' she insisted after she had greeted them warmly. 'Thank you so much for bringing the bike, Nick.' Fliss, eavesdropping, was surprised by the easy intimacy between her mother and the surgeon. Obviously they had done some pretty deep scheming up on the Heath the other day. 'Don't worry about Mortimer—now that you've said you'll work your magic on Matt it's in his interest to be thoroughly nice to you.'

Nick's raised eyebrows ventured to disagree, but Mrs Meredith was undeterred, and Fliss felt a vague sense of satisfaction that even the mighty Da Costa was able to be cowed by her dear old dad.

'You'd better go down the garden and say hallo to Biggles,' her mother went on regardless. 'He or she—or it, probably—is tethered down by the greenhouse; Matt insisted on bringing it up to see you, poor old thing,' she laughed.

'We can't miss this, can we?' Fliss manoeuvred Nick from the kitchen and out into the back garden, scarcely aware of the way she tugged his arm, or the movement of his hand on the back of her waist. Here at home her old fears and worries didn't apply. In her flat or at the hospital Nick's closeness might have seemed oppressive, inviting her body to betray itself. But in this relaxed atmosphere, their quiet intimacy seemed natural.

Matt zigzagged towards them across the lawn, applied his brakes and tumbled in slow motion to the ground. But he didn't utter the slightest word of complaint, merely picked up the bike and, asking them gruffly if they were going to see the pony, fell into step with them.

'Did you hurt yourself when you fell off? Did you feel the bump?'

Matt looked up at Nick amazed at such a banal question. 'I went bump,' was all he could think to say.

'I suppose his nervous system's all right?' Nick asked Fliss. 'He didn't seem to feel a thing.'

'You know, you are naïve, Mr Da Costa,' she laughed, looking up into his puzzled brown eyes. 'Matt doesn't think a bump like that's worth fussing about—and neither would any self-respecting ten-year-old. But because he's handicapped you reckon he ought to be wrapped in cotton wool and cry more easily. He's taken more bashes in his life than most other kids, haven't you, Matt?' Matt, still bemused, ran ahead.

'Biggles, Biggles! Here they are!' Contentedly munching grass, firmly tied by stout cord to the concrete post used normally to hoist the washing line, stood a fat New Forest pony, not very much larger than a large Great Dane.

'Hallo, Biggles,' they chorused in unison. The pony looked up for a moment, decided it was a lot of fuss about nothing and continued to eat.

'I can ride her,' boasted Matt, trying to haul himself up on to the broad back. The placid pony didn't raise its head from the grass. It had certainly been well chosen, Fliss reflected.

'Wait a moment. One, two three . . .' Nick took Matt firmly under the armpits and hoisted him aboard. The boy's legs scarcely found purchase around the rotund belly, but he smiled beatifically.

Nick took a peek at the relevant bits. 'You can tell your mother Biggles *is* an it,' he said mildly, coming back to where Fliss stood and putting his arm gently around her shoulder. It felt like the most natural thing in the world, and without thinking, eyes still on her brother on his perch, Fliss moved into Nick's side and found the warmth of him against her.

'Will you be all right having supper with Dad?' she asked quietly, aware of nothing but a glow of deep contentment. She slid her arm around his waist and pressed her hand to the warm flesh of his back through the shirt. He gave a little sigh, expressive of pleasure and resignation to the ordeal to come.

'I'll do my best,' he promised, his dark eyes seeming to absorb her as he took in her open, eager face and glowing cheeks. 'But don't ask me to go down on my knees and worship him, that's all. For you, though, I'll try.' He bent his head slowly and placed a light kiss on her forehead.

Matt, seated astride the complacent pony, watched with interest. Then he slid down the warm brown fur and hurried to Fliss's side. He seemed to say something and Fliss forsook the warmth of Nick's body to bend down to hear him. But he didn't speak. He reached up, placed his arms round her neck, and pressed a sticky kiss to the exact same spot Nick had just honoured. Touched almost to tears, Fliss kissed Matt's untroubled brow with equal gentleness.

'Thank you, darling,' she said quietly—and though Matt heard the words, Nick caught her glance and knew they were as much for him as for her small brother. Hand in hand, Matt in the middle, swinging high in the air between them, they made their way back to the house.

With Biddy and Mrs Meredith to divert any tense conversation, and with a fortuitous telephone call that claimed Sir Mortimer for half an hour, the meal went smoothly. Nick even found himself warming to the pleasant family atmosphere—with his mother dead for some years and his father based for tax purposes in Switzerland, it was a long time since he had known the simple pleasures of family conversation and several age groups engaged in a single task.

But by nine it was time to go, and well stocked up with freshly-made blackcurrant jam and crusty loaves, Nick and Fliss got into the sumptuous car and, waving until the last, drove away.

'Thank you.' Fliss, nervous now they were alone together, ran a light hand over his shoulder.

'I enjoyed it—well, most of it. I really did.' And he rested his hand on hers in her lap, and kept it there all the way back to Highstead, only removing it to change gear. It was nearly eleven when they arrived; Fliss had been wondering for the last ten minutes of the journey whether she should invite him in—but she knew what would happen if she did, and although part of her urged the invitation, something held back. Now she was really getting to know him, become really fond of him for what he was, not for what she imagined him to be, she didn't want to risk the friendship by losing it.

'I'd invite you in . . .' she started as he helped her out of the car and carried her bag laden with goodies to the front door.

'No, I don't think that would be wise,' he drawled cryptically, brushing her cheek with long, tapering fingers. 'You've been deep in thought all the way home, Fliss. Have you come to a decision?' He looked at her softly and she gazed back with those incandescent eyes that, for some reason, no longer seemed to pierce him as much as they once did. All he felt now was a dangerous, protective warmth with her there by him. 'Don't say no. Please, don't say no.' He whispered these words into her hair, holding her to him and threatening to rupture the thin plastic top of the jam-jar and cover the two of them with sticky jam.

'I'll take the job,' she murmured, suddenly shy of him in her arms, unable to look him in the eye. For the words declared far more than simple acceptance of a job offer. She was in love and she knew it; had realised it irrevocably this afternoon in the garden. And agreeing to work with this strange, wonderful man might mean heaven or hell for her, but at the moment she couldn't care less which, just so long as she could be with him.

'Marvellous girl,' he sighed, and his lips approached her own and took them in the sweetest, tenderest kiss she had known. 'That's enough for now,' he said at last, drawing himself away reluctantly. 'We have plenty of time tomorrow to talk.' He opened the door for her, saw she was safely inside—and, for the first time in close on thirty years, actually *skipped* down her garden path.

CHAPTER NINE

FLISS tripped into the senior staff common room on feet that felt as if they had wings. She had completed her morning tour of duty and spent an hour and a half with Sue, sorting out the piles of paperwork and arranging for important things to be sent down to Barney so that he could okay them. Nigel was due to arrive back at work tomorrow, which disappointed Fliss in a way because it would mean that there was no need for her and Nick to work together on the list. But Nick, she knew, was very busy indeed and would be pleased to have the workload lifted . . . And anyway, it wouldn't be long before they could work together permanently.

Fliss had seen him briefly this morning, but he had given her only a vague wave as he had escorted a distinguished-looking man down the corridor to his office. He was interviewing for most of the week, trying to find suitable staff, from junior nurses to surgeons and anaesthetists. Junior nurses . . . Fliss felt a twinge of discomfort as she remembered that the pretty young nurse on Kate's ward would be transferring to the Seymour unit too. Would they both end up discarded by a man who seemed to have a penchant for loving and leaving perfectly good women? Though she knew now, without a doubt, that the perpetual butterflies in her stomach and the confidence that she could do anything were love, real love, Fliss was still wise enough to acknowledge that there were far more suitable men than Nick Da Costa to get involved with. Nick wasn't the kind of man who looked for anything permanent, and even if he did seem to have changed in the last couple of days with her there was no guarantee that it was going to last. How she wished she could trust him completely! But at the back of her mind the fear of betrayal, and the knowledge he had let down a dozen or more equally enamoured ladies, still rankled and wouldn't be soothed, except by his presence. Would a relationship with him be like this all the time? Fliss wondered. Even though she loved him, would she still have to spend every hour when he wasn't there with her worrying about what he was doing—and with whom? Perhaps there was something to be said for solid, reliable men like Peter after all . . .

Peter and Kate were peering at the announcement pinned to the common room board. 'What's up?' asked Fliss, approaching them.

'Sister Mac's leaving this Friday—we've got to get our contributions for her present to Theatre Sister Arnold by tomorrow. How much does the old girl merit, Fliss?' Kate asked facetiously.

'It's a shame,' Peter shrugged. 'I know she's a bit tough on the nurses, but they're certainly very well trained once she's had her time with them. She's the last of her generation of Sisters at the hospital, you know. Things won't be the same again.'

'And when are you off?' asked Fliss, sensing that it was his own departure that had brought on this sudden gloom.

'End of the month—and I'm going to Corfu for a fortnight after that,' he brightened. 'I've been trying to persuade Kate to take a break and come with me. And how about you, Fliss?' He looked at her enquiringly. Any other time, any other circumstances, Fliss might have welcomed a holiday in congenial company. But now she had a perfect excuse for declining the offer.

'I've got some news myself, actually,' she admitted. 'I've been offered a job on the Seymour team and I've accepted, so I won't be able to have a holiday this year, more's the pity.'

Kate and Peter both raised eyebrows that expressed complete knowledge of what had happened yesterday. 'Told you!' Kate crowed. 'What did he have to do to persuade you?'

'Nothing—the job speaks for itself. And I seem to remember that it wasn't so long ago that we discussed the situation and you told me to do whatever I had to for it!' Fliss protested archly. 'Some friend you are, Kate!'

'Bearing in mind that it wasn't so long ago that Da Costa stood in this very room and swore he'd die rather than offer you a job, I quite understand Kate's confusion,' said Peter, laughing with the irony of it all. 'How temperamental you surgeons are! I'm glad I won't have to deal with your egos for very much longer. How's Barney, by the way—speaking of monumental egos?'

'Well enough to be thoroughly fed up with his awful children and volunteering to come back to do what he can. He'll be able to do all the paperwork with Sue's help, which'll take some of the pressure off Nigel and me. And I suppose that he could take an outpatients clinic or two, with a bit of a back-up.'

'If any of you care to give me a donation for Sister Mac I'll take it down to Theatres after lunch,' Peter offered. 'The party's on Friday evening, I see. I wonder what we can buy her to make her retirement fulfilled?'

'An electric wok,' suggested Kate, knowing full well that Sister was not at all keen on anything that wasn't good English or Scots fare.

'A set of satin underwear . . .' 'Too frivolous! How about an exercise bike?' With silly suggestions in the air, the three of them went off for lunch together.

'He's been in here how long?' Fliss had been called along to Men's Medical to check on an ulcer case who had been brought in for medical stabilisation but who had deteriorated badly since his admission. Sister was a young woman, recently promoted, who didn't seem to have everything at her fingertips yet.

'Er . . . I don't seem to have his admission date on here . . . Staff Nurse, run and fetch Mr Allaway's notes from the office, will you?' She turned, embarrassed, to Fliss, who tried to pretend that the delay hadn't happened.

'And you're in worse pain now, Mr Allaway, than you were when you were admitted?' Fliss asked quietly, her stethoscope checking his heart. He was tense, obviously in discomfort.

'They took me off the drugs I was used to,' he said with some effort, 'and I got worse very quickly. I don't understand why I couldn't keep on with my old treatment.'

'I'm afraid I'm not in the position to be able to explain it to you, either,' Fliss explained carefully. The ways of the medics were sometimes beyond her; but she supposed they had had a reason for doing such a thing.

Mr Allaway's notes arrived, carried by a sweating, very plump staff nurse who was beginning to wilt in the afternoon heat which had sent half the patients off to sleep. Apart from the odd giggle and scrape from the direction of the ward office and sluice, the place was almost silent. Fliss and Sister suited their voices to the atmosphere, talking almost in whispers. It was the sort of July afternoon when the only thing to do was to go and sleep in the shade in a garden, to the buzzing of bees and the occasional chirp of a hyperactive bird who didn't know the meaning of *siesta*.

Fliss went through the notes and took the X-rays back to the office for a minute to have a close look at them. 'Right, Mr Allaway,' she said at last, 'if your doctor agrees we'll take you down to theatre first thing tomorrow morning and have a look at this ulcer of yours. What do you know about it?'

'Not very much,' he admitted sheepishly. 'Will it hurt more if I have it done?'

Resigned to a long explanation of the process of removing a duodenal ulcer, Fliss pulled the chair up from the end of his bed and sat down. 'There's no need to stay, Sister,' she said. 'But if you could contact Dr Price so that we can get this made official, I'd be grateful.' And Sister hurried off.

Nick or no Nick, in love or not, work came first. And if her smile was brighter and her heart full to overflowing with pleasure, few people noticed it that busy afternoon as she did her consent rounds and checked up on her old patients.

'I really think we can say goodbye to Mrs Morrissey soon,' Sister Slater announced as Fliss arrived on Women's Surgical. 'She's very much better, and I had a chat with her husband last night and he's fixed up a fortnight's holiday for her—a nice hotel in Frinton—for next week. How do you feel about letting her go?'

'She'll have to be a bit careful about what she eats. Is she still on a low residue diet?' Fliss frowned a little. Sometimes a patient's nearest and dearest, though well-meaning, could be their own worst enemies.

'Yes, but I've been adding more substance recently

and she's coping perfectly,' Sister responded. 'We could do with the bed and she's very bored here.'

'I do believe you're determined to see her go, Sister,' Fliss smiled. 'And if you reckon it's time to say goodbye to her, I'm not going to fuss.'

And indeed, Mrs Morrissey was very much better looking, with more colour and a steady blood pressure—and, she insisted, bored out of her mind.

'Sister here has persuaded me that I have to open the bars and let you go,' grinned Fliss. 'I hear you're going to Frinton. Just make sure you don't do anything too energetic, won't you? Shall we say Friday, then, so that you can be at home for the weekend? And meanwhile, Sister, would you ensure that the dietician and the physiotherapist both give Mrs Morrissey hints on how to cope at home for the next few months.'

'That's wonderful!' beamed Mrs Morrissey. 'Thanks ever so much, dear. I'm feeling right as rain, if only I could get off this bed.'

'Just be warned,' Fliss went on, hating to sound such a killjoy, 'that you've been in it for several weeks now. Your legs aren't used to the exercise and nor is the rest of you. You'll feel as weak as a baby once you're at home. I hope that husband of yours realises he'll be doing the cooking and cleaning for a while yet!'

'He does, don't you worry,' the patient assured the surgeon. 'And I'll soon let him know if he starts expecting too much.'

'Good for you, then,' and Fliss made her exit.

Mrs Nicholls was quite back to her old self and tried not to show too much disappointment that it was Fliss who had come to see her rather than the gorgeous Mr Da Costa, to whom she was becoming rather attached.

'I'm afraid he's a very busy man,' Fliss explained while Sister unwound the dressing and allowed the wound to be seen. The bruising had gone down quite well, but still Mrs Nicholls didn't care to see it.

'Raise your arm for me, please.' She did so, with a deal of discomfort. 'And now stretch it out and point your fingers.' Fliss checked for any undue pull on the scar and found that there wasn't any, which sent a tingle of pride through her. Then she sat down and discussed arrangements for radiotherapy follow-up. 'The prospects are really excellent for you,' she was able to assure the patient. 'We caught you early and the lymph glands weren't affected. This is just the belt-and-braces procedure to ensure that we don't have you coming back for more of the same.'

'I assure you, I won't,' Mrs Nicholls said with feeling. But she seemed in good spirits, willing to do whatever was required to ensure recovery, and Fliss left her reading a magazine and looking quite contented with the way things had turned out.

Sister Slater offered tea in her office and then had to disappear to show another surgeon round the ward. Fliss glanced at her watch. It was three-thirty. She would go home now for a couple of hours while visitors were around and pop back later for a while to ensure that everything was all right. Informing Sue of her plans so that, if necessary, she could be contacted at home, Fliss made her way out. Passing her pigeonhole, she found a note on Nick's hand-made paper.

Interviews all afternoon, sorry I missed you at lunch. I'll call on you about eight, okay? Nick.

Not *love* Nick, or *ever yours*, Nick . . . But then, Fliss decided, trundling up the hill and into the little Asian grocer's for milk and eggs, open demonstration of his feelings wasn't really a part of Nick's character. Some-times a spark of dissent flashed out to leave people reeling, but more often than not his thoughts were hidden behind those glittering dark eyes and that gloriously curvy mouth. Well, if she had to leave him a note, would she put all her cards on the table? No, she decided, making herself another pot of tea and carrying it to the open window of the sitting-room to rest with her feet up for a few minutes before tackling the washing. No, she wouldn't risk that.

'Miss Meredith!' It was ten past seven. Fliss had spent a while in confab with Mr Allaway's doctor, who wasn't very keen on his patient having surgery even though he was in pain, and Fliss had had to call in a senior opinion from one of the other teams to back her up; Mr Allaway would be first on the morrow's operating list. She was just making her way through the outpatients department when a nurse came tearing up.

'Miss Meredith! Will you go to Casualty, please! We've just had an emergency admitted—too bad to be taken on to Bart's . . .'

Though she knew she was due to meet Nick, Fliss didn't hesitate. She ran, which was quite improper, to the treatment room set aside for those patients ill or injured enough to ignore the sign at the hospital gate declaring that 'This hospital does not have a Casualty Department.'

A little girl lay gasping on the couch, the duty officer, a doctor, bending over her. He looked up and saw who had just entered.

'Bleach,' he said simply.

'Hell!' exclaimed Fliss. Every month or so they had one—a child curious enough to persist in downing bleach or cleaning fluid or paint stripper, despite the taste and smell of the stuff. 'Tracheotomy?'

'Yes, we've rinsed her out, but the oedema is beginning to make her breathing very difficult.'

'Get her to theatre—and keep that tube down her as long as you can,' Fliss instructed, pointing to the tube that had been used for the stomach rinse and which protruded from the child's mouth.

The team in theatre was very definitely gathered from scratch. There was a young anaesthetist who was obviously scared stiff of administering an intravenous anaesthetic to a child and had to keep consulting his tables, and an equally nervous theatre staff nurse, who had managed to lay up the tray wrongly. Fliss waited more and more impatiently as valuable minutes were lost; eventually, it was the junior nurse, the unscrubbed assistant, who managed to track down the source of tracheal dilators and McIndoe's forceps that were necessary.

'I'm going to report this to Sister McIlvaney first thing tomorrow,' she said vindictively, watching them both start like frightened rabbits. 'Not because I want to see you two get into hot water but because, before she leaves us for good, I'd like to feel sure that everyone in theatre can lay up a tracheostomy tray,' she softened the blow, calling the operation by its official title.

With the child ready, they started. It wasn't a difficult operation in itself, really; nevertheless, it was gone nine by the time they had finished and the girl was in the recovery room, her breathing assisted by a respirator.

'I think we'll try to track down Mr Da Costa,' Fliss decided as the child was wheeled away. 'He's our burns expert.' But Nick wasn't at his home number and he failed to respond to his bleeper. Fliss at last admitted defeat and called out another doctor before changing out of her gown and going back to the reception area and trying to explain to the mother, a good five years younger than herself, what had happened. But she seemed to take very little notice of Fliss's description of the damage and repairs and dangers involved.

All she kept saying was, 'I *knew* if I left it there she'd have it, I knew it all along . . .'

Fliss refrained from asking why on earth the woman had left the bleach there if she'd been so certain her child would drink it—but there was no point in being sanctimonious now that the little girl had suffered so badly. There was no knowing what might happen— whether her stomach or vocal chords would be damaged, whether she had arrived in hospital in time. Instead, she just escorted the woman up to Intensive Care, where the child would be transferred, and left her wringing her hands as she waited outside.

Nick would be there, on her front wall, legs dangling while he waited patiently for her—she *knew* he would as she jogged up the hill in the still, oppressive air that presaged another thunderstorm. Where else could he be? He wasn't at his home number, gleaned from theatre records; he wasn't in the hospital . . . Fliss rounded the corner to the house with an expectant smile on her face. But there was no big BMW in the kerb and no good-looking man perched on the wall. Nor was there a note through the letterbox. Fliss let herself in, dialled his home number again, and again through the evening. And then, giving up in frustration, she went to have a bath—and while she was splashing away her woes in the tub, full of her favourite foaming oil, the phone rang.

Clad only in a towel, Fliss raced to the receiver—but it was only one of Jane's friends who had been unable to contact Jane and wanted to know if he could dump a rug that she had bought at the house. Fliss agreed to take the carpet for him; he came; she phoned Nick again . . . And finally, at gone midnight, wishing she had had the sense to leave a trail of notes all over their patch of London so that Nick couldn't believe she had stood him up again, Fliss went miserably to bed.

She woke at seven to an overcast, misty day and got up with a feeling of dread that she couldn't quite pin down. Ready early, and hearing Jane's footsteps above, Fliss decided to deliver the rug, a pastel-coloured dhurri to go with Jane's high-tec decorating style, herself—and perhaps scrounge a cup of coffee off a sympathetic soul in the process. With the rug's bulk under one arm, she climbed the stairs, knocked on the door and waited a minute. When Jane didn't answer, Fliss gently turned the handle; it moved and the door opened, and with a lighthearted cry of, 'Wakey, wakey!' she burst into Jane's sitting-room.

Except that it wasn't Jane who was just emerging from the direction of the bathroom; it was Nick Da Costa, wearing no more than a bath towel and obviously just out of the shower.

'Good morning,' he said in a gruff sort of voice that told her he hadn't been up for very long.

Fliss was so stunned to find him there that for a few moments she was absolutely speechless while her mind began to click almost automatically through all the reasons why he was here. And they all led to one answer; Jane herself. He had betrayed her, Fliss knew with a sinking certainty that made her want to burst into tears and simultaneously made her stomach lurch with revulsion.

'Where's Jane?' she asked steadily, looking around the place with its stripped floors and squared-off, hideously uncomfortable seating. The flat was unnaturally tidy, as always; Jane had a place for everything and everything in its place—and that included Nick Da Costa in her bed, it was obvious.

'She had to go,' Nick replied casually, tucking his towel around him firmly before he dared to move. 'Come and have some coffee,' he suggested in that unintentionally seductive voice. 'I put some on to perk while I took a shower. What's wrong?'

Fliss's anguished eyes flew over the wide expanse of chest where water droplets still glistened among the dark hair, took in his flat stomach, his neat navel, the wavy line of masculinity that arrowed down into the regions hidden by his towel. He had a day and a night's growth of beard making him look more impossibly handsome than ever . . . so rakish, debauched. She felt tears on her lashes and an unbearable numbness creeping through her at what he had done.

'How can you ask that?' she cried, her pain lacing every word, her distraught mouth pleading with him as he watched her draw her hand over her face. 'How can you spend the night with my friend in the flat above mine, and just offer me a cup of coffee? Oh, *Nick!*'

Unable to see where she was going, she turned in the direction she thought she had come in, searching wildly for the door handle, which was on the side of the door opposite to her own downstairs. A sob fought to make itself heard in the back of her throat and she swallowed it down with a rasping breath. How could he have done this to her? Was it revenge for something she'd done?

Perhaps it was just because of who she was, she thought frenziedly, trying to tug the door open—but the latch had slipped down and she fought to release it . . .

Suddenly strong arms were around her and Nick pulled her back from her flight. 'Fliss darling, what's wrong?' She struggled in his arms and for the first time really knew the strength of him as he refused to free her, pinioned her arms, turned her forcibly to face him.

Fliss kicked, and her leather pump made contact with his bare shin—but though he cursed he seemed determined not to release her, and when she looked up into his face it wasn't fury or revenge she saw there, but genuine fear of something, and concern that had made his face pale under his tan. At last he had her still; they both stood, breathing heavily.

'Just let me out, that's all I want,' she said at last. 'I'll resign from the unit first thing, if you've gone so far as to make my appointment official.'

'Is this all in aid of last night?' he asked incredulously, confusion racing across his classical features. 'Good lord, Fliss—you're in the business yourself! You can't always expect me to be a hundred per cent reliable.'

'Reliable!' The tears welled up again; tears at the realisation that it all meant so little to him. That the little matter of him sleeping with Jane was a matter of reliability, not of morals or love . . . No, certainly not of love. How could a man like Nicholas Da Costa, libertine that he was, know anything of love? 'Just let me go. I don't want to see you again,' was all she could sob—and then his hand was cradling her head to his shoulder and the clean smell of his skin was in her nostrils, and all she wanted was just to die like this, to be swept into oblivion while his fingers caressed her neck and his throaty early-morning voice whispered endearments and the length of his firm body, so masterful, so masculine, so full of life and promise, pressed against her, offering all the promise in the world, should she only reach out for it. But he was a liar, a womaniser, a man who held relationships lightly, and her spirit, fanned to glowing warmth by his ardour, exploded again into flames of indignation.

'Stop it, please stop it!' She jerked her head away from his magical hands and succeeded in pushing him back a few steps—and this time he stood back, his breathing ragged, his confusion—oh, what an excellent actor he was!—evident for her to see in his glowing eyes and tense mouth.

'Fliss, whatever it is, I'm sorry. I know we didn't manage to see each other last night, but Jane . . .' he started, but Fliss cut in.

'Don't mention her to me. How could you, Nick? I'd just begun to think I was in love with you; I'd started to believe that you cared. And now this!' She moved his arm, which had come out to detain her, away and walked slowly to the door. 'You know, I was absolutely right when I told you that you'd ruined my life—you had. And if this is your idea of being grown up you can keep it. I don't want any of it. It's all just a big game as far as you're concerned, isn't it?' He looked at her across the few feet that divided them with something like desperation in his eyes as her words sank in.

'Anyway,' she turned the door handle, 'you've got what you wanted. You've shattered my innocence, if that's what it's called these days, you've made me look a fool and you've disrupted my career . . .' She didn't add that he'd broken her heart, because she had given him that without a request—and her heart was her own responsibility.

'Marry me. Marry me, Fliss.' Nick's words scarcely made an impression on her as she turned on to the landing. 'You heard what I said. I love you. Let's get married.' The words came involuntarily to his tongue, so completely alien to him that they sounded like a foreign language. But just at that moment he knew that he'd said the right thing—that he wanted nothing in the world more than this woman, shaken and hurt in front of him, for whatever reason, to be his to care for ever. '*Please*,' he added, as she turned again to go downstairs. 'Fliss, I mean it. *Marry me!*'

'Not if you were the last man on earth,' she said quietly as she returned to her own flat. 'How could you possibly know what marriage means?'

His grim face, white-lipped, brow furrowed, as he leaned over the banister in his towel, was the last she saw of him.

CHAPTER TEN

MARRY me . . . I love you . . . What the hell did he know about love? Fliss asked herself repetitively as she threw together the things she would need for the day and stormed out of the house, Nick's taunting words ringing resoundingly in her ears. She was scarcely safe to cross the road, for the last thing her mind was on was the traffic pouring down the hill and into central London, but with her mind still awhirl she made it safely to the hospital.

Just thank God Nigel was here and would be doing today's list, she thought desperately, trying to settle herself over a cup of coffee in the senior staff room. But it was impossible to blank out what had just happened. Her heart was still thumping away nineteen to the dozen, she still had a pang of nausea deep inside—and all she wanted to do was to get away from this place and hide; make a burrow for herself somewhere away from all this noise and the familiar reminders of what a fool she'd been and just teach herself to cope with the aching knowledge of what had happened. Nick had betrayed her by spending a night with Jane—and then he had had the total insensitivity to ask her, Fliss, to marry him . . .

She rested her face in her hands and tried to suck in enough air to drown the awful betraying wail that threatened to break out. So this was what the other nurses had been suffering from when he ditched them; this was what it was to arrive at work feeling as if you couldn't go on for a minute longer. Feeling the real physical pain of heart that had, until now, been a myth that Fliss had pooh-poohed. Love couldn't hurt, she had laughingly told Kate who had had a bad time with an understanding young Oxford medical student—who had been gone off to be understanding to someone else. But oh, it *did* hurt! It hurt like a knife twisted between the ribs, like a gall bladder operation on the wrong side . . .

'Fliss! Aren't you pleased to see me? What on earth's been happening while I've been away?' Nigel, pinkly tanned despite his reddish hair that promised freckles and not much more, came stomping in at that moment and caught her unawares.

'Nigel—just look at you!' she managed to respond, though it took a deal of effort. 'How's married life? I hope it's all right for this morning, too—it's a fairly light list . . .'

'Married life is wonderful,' he began, and watched her face crumple as she tried not to let the words penetrate further than her ears. Married life wonderful? Married life with Nick Da Costa notching up his conquests on the nuptial bed . . . Could that ever be wonderful?

'What's the matter?' Nigel took the chair at her side and, in his fussy fashion, bent an arm carefully around her to shield her from non-existent prying eyes. 'It must have been terribly tough for you, Fliss, what with Barney having his accident and this new chap just walking in and taking over from you . . .'

'It wasn't like that,' Fliss butted in, irrationally coming to the defence of the man she had been steeling herself to hate. 'We wouldn't have managed without him, and I've been doing most of the basics.' She sighed and shook off Nigel's paternal arm. 'I'm just terribly tired, that's all. I could do with three weeks in the Caribbean. What was it like, eh? All blue skies and warm water and soft silver

sand? Or nasty things that bit and food that had you
locked in the loo for a week?'

'Some of each,' he laughed a little forcedly. 'Come on,
let's go down to theatre and I'll tell you all about it.' And
in his rather old fashioned but charming way he led her
out. 'How did you manage to get Barney to break his
leg?' his voice floated back down the hall. 'Sister's
retiring too—and I've heard the most absurd rumour
that Peter Locke is going too—the place seems to have
undergone a revolution in my absence!'

As a surgeon Nigel was so meticulous as to drive
almost everyone mad. He worked slowly and very carefully, like a hairdresser who snips, combs this way,
combs that, snips again, leaves it a minute and then
comes back . . . The nursing staff hated all the standing
around doing nothing while he surveyed what he had
just done from every angle. Anaesthetists—not, this
morning, thank goodness, Peter—hated having to keep
the patient under for longer than strictly necessary. And
the assistant surgeon spent most of her time offering
mild information and advice, stooping to inspect an
incision, debating with him whether it would be necessary to suture here or there and just waiting for the
moment when she would be allowed to close up.

Normally a steady, careful worker, Fliss was like the
Steve Ovett of the operating theatre that morning. Yet,
when she considered it, she didn't know which approach
was best—that quick, get in there and do it attitude of
Barney's, which had led to Mrs Morrissey being brought
back for repair, or Nigel's belt-and-braces technique.
Neither was ideal, Fliss thought, her eyes welling with
tears as she reached out for another suture in its holder,
passed to her by the scrubbed assistant. Nick Da Costa's
approach was as near to perfection as she could imagine;

speed, versatility, yet the patience to instil confidence into someone not absolutely certain what they were doing. She blinked once or twice to clear her eyes and cleared her throat with a little cough.

'Not sickening for something, are you, Miss Meredith?' came Sister McIlvaney's request. 'Not only is it very bad for the patient, but I had hoped you'd be coming along to the wee party I'm holding in honour of my retirement.'

'That's very kind of you,' Fliss replied, pleased to have something else to talk and think about; she didn't normally have any problem about cutting herself off from the real world when she was working, but today . . .

'It's to be on Friday,' Sister said as if she was announcing the day the dustmen came, a fact that had very little bearing on her life. 'I dare say there'll be the odd drop of champagne to tempt you young ones along.'

'The hospital won't be able to run without you,' protested Nigel. 'There'll be insurrection within the walls in days. You'll have to come back, Sister, every now and then, to remind people of how things really should be done.'

Despite her bulk, Sister preened. 'Och, I don't know if we'll have time for that, you know! We're going on one of these long winter holidays in November—two months on the Costa Brava—so I don't suppose I'll have time to come back and check up on all of you.'

Was that a flicker of relief that Fliss saw cross the junior nurses' faces? Yet give them a month without Sister and a bit of promotion and they'd soon be moaning about how standards had fallen since their day and how no one knew about how to teach discipline any more!

The morning's surgery was over—it was nearly two, even though it had been a light list—and there weren't many people in the theatre who hadn't noticed how strained and preoccupied Miss Meredith was.

'It's because she won't be operating with Mr Da Costa any more,' one of the junior nurses had been heard saying to another. 'Just because she's got letters to her name it doesn't mean she hasn't got a heart, you know. And I heard that they spent the weekend together—so he's obviously given her the push, like he did Karen . . .'

Nigel was equally aware that something was wrong, but he didn't have the same knowledge to explain why. Nevertheless, as they finished their tour of the recovery room and saw a couple of patients back up to the ward, he said sympathetically, 'Why don't you take a couple of days off, Fliss? Go away, get some fresh air and sleep and come back on, say, Friday. We've got nothing impossible on, have we?'

'There's a small intestinal list for tomorrow,' she said wearily. 'I admitted them yesterday. And there's the big outpatient clinic on Thursday morning . . . I don't think I can leave you to that, Nigel. I know from bitter experience what it's like.' But oh, how wonderful it would be to get away from all this, to have time to herself to cry and to think and not to be perpetually bottling it up, aware of everyone's pity.

'I'll get Barney in for Thursday—you said he wanted to come in for Outpatients. And I'll cope tomorrow. I'm not taking no for an answer, do you hear?'

'But Nigel, you've just got back from honeymoon— your wife won't want you wilted by the time you get home . . .'

Nigel gave her the oddest look and she giggled a bit at what she'd just said. 'You're exhausted,' he insisted.

'Go home now; I'll do the follow-ups and I'll check with Barney and the powers that be. Just scat, Fliss—and don't show your face until Friday morning!'

Where could a woman on her own, in need of peace and solitude, escape for two days? Fliss packed a bag with a vague idea forming in her mind; she would go somewhere warm near the sea; somewhere not too tame and crowded, somewhere she could walk until she dropped and forget Nick Da Costa's betrayal in the oblivion of exhausted sleep. Memories of a childhood holiday on Dartmoor came back to her; she knew the place.

Without leaving a note and with only the briefest of falsely cheerful phone calls to assure her mother that she hadn't disappeared off the face of the earth, Fliss grabbed her mail and a book and a box of tissues and, just five hours later—for she'd missed a train at Paddington—alighted at Exeter. From there in a hired car she drove across country to Chagford and from there on to the moor proper—and yes, there it was, just as she remembered; a low-built stone farmhouse surrounded by outbuildings and advertising bed and breakfast for the knowledgeable few who left the wide roads for the distinctly Cornish lanes that twisted and narrowed alarmingly.

There was a bed for the night and for the next three in a large room with a sloping floor and a chest of drawers in which not a drawer would open. And there was peace, quiet and a filling meal from the farmer's wife, even though Fliss had arrived well after the usual time for visitors. And, through the dimming mists of time, they even pretended to remember her as a child, coming down with her parents and Biddy for a week each summer.

The days flew by and with each, thoughts of Nick began to fall into perspective. On Tuesday he was still a digging pain and a single thought of him could reduce her to impotent tears of rage and disappointment that such a man could have let her, and himself, down so badly. But on Wednesday, after another night's sleep and a day spent out walking on the eerie, Neolithic-tombed spaces of the moor, he had become a memory—a painful one, something she would rather not think about, like an embarrassing public experience or a childhood fright. And on Thursday, out for a ride with the Chagford riding school and then for the hour's drive to the coast to breathe in soporific sea air, a scab had grown over the wound Nick had made. Now it was protected from the air; the hurt was no longer so sharp, though a dull, distrustful ache continued to beat in her breast and she knew that it would be a long time, if ever, before she allowed another man to come close enough to do what he had done again. Strong, tanned, fortified and with thoughts of revenge already asserting themselves, as they had to if she was to survive in the same hospital, Fliss headed reluctantly back to London on Thursday evening.

Nothing had changed in her absence, as she rather hoped it might. The garden was still overgrown, the sun still shining, the traffic still streaming up the hill; and as she entered the house Fliss felt a frisson of sadness and perplexity come over her. But she steeled herself and made a welcoming pot of tea, flinging the windows wide and allowing the sunshine into her favourite room as she sat on the sofa and drank two great mugfuls of the brew. There was a pile of post to be opened, most of it bumf from medical firms and bills. Instinct warning her off the brown envelopes with official symbols on the front, Fliss reached for an innocent-looking cream one and carelessly tore it open.

Congratulations! she read. *You have won our Carachoc Bar Anniversary Competition.* Fliss paused—it must be a mistake. She couldn't remember even filling out the form—damn it, she hadn't even known the answers . . . But Nick Da Costa had, hadn't he? He must have picked the slip of paper up that day he'd ridiculed her in the common room, filled it out and posted it off—with *her* name on the form. She scanned down the gushing prose; a year's supply of Chewies she could do without, but a car she'd like very much. And what Nick Da Costa didn't know about, the toad, Nick Da Costa wouldn't miss. She would have no compunction about accepting a car and damning him to hell.

We are proud to present you with your choice of holiday for two in a luxury hotel in Indonesia. Choose from any of the islands, including the delights of exotic Bali, with its miles of sandy beaches and intriguing culture . . .

'A holiday for two!' Fliss's cry rang from the ceiling. What would she want with a romantic holiday for two on Bali? It was too cruel a jibe. But it must be worth a couple of thousand pounds, mustn't it, she thought quickly. Perhaps they'd give her the cash instead and she could buy a secondhand car . . .

The slam of the front door was instantly followed by a bashing on her own. Fliss got up to answer.

Jane flew into the room like a bat out of hell. 'Felicity Meredith, you coot!' she screeched, taking Fliss firmly by the shoulders and giving her a mild shake. 'Where on earth have you been? We were all worried sick about you! We all thought you'd run away to do yourself in until Nick had the bright idea of phoning your mother. What are you playing at, dashing around the country with hardly a word of explanation to your friends?'

Fliss could hardly think. 'Hallo, Jane,' she said finally. 'Would you like a cup of tea?'

It wasn't Jane's fault that Nick had used her; it wasn't Jane's fault that she'd fallen for Nick's suave good looks and been taken in by his treacherous patter. But somehow Fliss wasn't in the mood to be too lenient on her friend from upstairs. It took two to tango, and if Jane had been unwilling then . . . Well, then perhaps this whole sordid mess would never have happened.

'No, not tea. But I've got some explaining to do,' Jane said anxiously, sensing Fliss's reserve and guessing why. She drew the reluctant surgeon back to the sofa and sat her down. 'You think that Nick and I spent Monday night upstairs together, don't you?' she said without preamble.

'Are you going to tell me you didn't?' Fliss asked coldly. 'It's a bit difficult to deny it, Jane, when I found him up there dressed in your bath towel and offering me a cup of your coffee.'

'You're an absolute, innocent fool, do you know that?' Jane roared with laughter. 'I admit I fancied Nick like hell; I even gave him my front door key so that he could come up if he wanted to without too much fuss of arranging a meeting—I know what odd hours you surgeons work and I thought that if he availed himself of my flat when he found himself with a few hours off, he might avail himself of me, too.'

'And did he?' asked Fliss carefully, reluctantly, almost afraid of what she was going to hear yet needing desperately to know.

'I wish he had, but he didn't. I spent Monday night out

on the tiles and when I got back on Tuesday evening there was a polite note from him saying he'd spent the night on the sofa and a couple of quid to cover laundry and food. I ask you,' Jane pulled a face, 'it's not exactly romantic, is it? I feel as if I'm running a bed and breakfast establishment rather than a passion parlour!'

'He could have told me as much himself,' sputtered Fliss, unwilling to be duped a second time. 'Come clean with me, Jane, and admit that this is just a cover-up job to save him being caught with his pants down.' She smiled as the picture of him almost naked, wrapped only in that bath towel, came back to her. He wasn't wearing any pants at the time to pull down!

'I have a confession to make.' Jane looked as contrite as she could. 'When I gave him my key I said I'd make it clear to you what I'd done and that it was merely a considerate gesture. But . . . Well, you've already heard about the ulterior motive. I didn't mean to deceive you, Fliss, but I just rather hoped . . . I'm sorry. You've been thinking I'm a real bitch, I know. But I came to feel resentful for the hold you had over him . . .'

'The hold *I* had over him?' Fliss echoed incredulously. '*Me?* This *is* a put-up job!' She crossed her knees, though, wanting to hear every last detail. Somewhere deep inside a flicker of hope, unquenchable and probably the forerunner to disaster, was beginning to rise.

'All he seemed to think about all the time we were out together was you,' Jane confessed with a blush. 'It was obvious from the start that we'd got each other pretty well sussed out, but I couldn't believe it when he started asking about you. What were you like, did you have lots of money and boy-friends, what did I know about your reputation at the hospital . . . All that kind of thing. And we got back here all right and I was rather looking forward to . . .' She blushed even pinker and avoided Fliss's clear eye. 'Well, you know, getting to know him better . . .' Fliss raised a cool eyebrow, surprised that the liberated Jane was not quite as sophisticated as she seemed. Half of her wanted to hear all about it; hear the details of what she had missed; hear Jane confirm that Nick was a superb lover.

'And?' she asked gently.

'We got upstairs and everything was fine for a few minutes, but then as soon as I hinted at bed he cooled off—if he'd ever been turned on, that is! Kept muttering about you getting the wrong idea—said anyway he was tired, and soon after that he cleared off home.' Jane picked a non-existent fleck of dust off her knee. 'So there you are! My first rejection for a very long time, I assure you, and I've got no intention of letting it happen again. He didn't want anything to do with me because of what I was or who I was—he just wanted to know all about you.'

Fliss leant over and hugged her, the flicker of hope bursting spontaneously into flame in her breast. 'Why was he here the other night?' she asked as she let Jane go.

'Oh, it was all something to do with an emergency and not wanting to wake you up . . . I didn't understand it and he was in a state; we couldn't find you anywhere and he couldn't understand why you'd told him to go to hell because he thought you knew he had a key. You'll have to see him to get all the facts.' Jane stood up, relief and slight loss of face expressed in her shoulders. 'Just you play your cards right this time, that's all I'm telling you. I'd have done anything to get him interested, and you only call him names and give him a chocolate biscuit and he's eating out of your hand—you lucky, lucky thing!'

Fliss's plans to arrive early at the hospital and seek Nick out were shot down before they could even begin—for worn out by the emotional upheaval and the travelling she managed to oversleep. Not disastrously, thank goodness, because there was no surgery today, but late enough to mean that she could not waste time going to look for him when he was likely to be tied up with business for the unit.

The morning she spent exultantly bestowing unprovoked smiles on the patients in the small outpatient clinic she had been delegated to run; and while some sufferers were delighted at their breezy treatment, others complained that they were not treated with quite the gravity and gloomy prognosis that they had come to expect when they brought their ulcers or their prolapses to the doctors. Once, as the door opened and the clinic nurse ushered in the next pained patient, Fliss caught a glimpse of Nick waiting nonchalantly outside, looking disgustingly fit and lean and tanned in comparison with the wincing paleness of her clients. He had seen her, raised a hand and exchanged a long, intense look which seemed to tell her that he wanted to talk to her at length about something later . . . But then the nurse had come in with the next case and the door had divided them.

At lunch time Fliss phoned his room, but there was no answer and her call was transferred to an assistant involved on the Seymour unit, who apologisingly admitted that Mr Da Costa had been called away for lunch with the contractors but would be back later.

Fliss prowled the corridors with Nigel as they did a ward round with her eyes searching for a glimpse of that familiar tall, straight, infinitely attractive figure, but she saw nothing of him and her heart lurched again. Was hope to have been encouraged so cruelly, only to be doused again?

Mrs Morrissey's discharge papers were signed—Nigel let Fliss do it, refusing in his gentlemanly fashion to take credit for a job he had not been involved in—and they bade a cheerful goodbye, Fliss feeling a surge of real pride, for Mrs Morrissey was one of the first patients she had had complete responsibility for. Mrs Hudd was also dismissed, having made a steady recovery, and Mrs Nicholls was given permission to leave the hospital for a few hours on Sunday to go to a christening, only on the proviso that she take it easy and come straight back.

'It's amazing how a sympathetic surgeon can aid a patient's recovery,' Nigel said aloud. 'Mastectomy usually leaves them depressed and lacking confidence, but this selective operation seems to conquer those enemies of recovery.'

'Let's try making the point to Barney,' Fliss said seriously. 'The operation takes a little longer, maybe, but it's a good investment.'

'Okay,' Nigel agreed. 'As soon as he's on his feet we'll stage a fait accompli and demand a more sympathetic attitude! And now how about going down and drowning our sorrows with Sister Mac's champagne?'

The party was well under way when they arrived and Sister herself greeted them at the door; but Fliss's words of sorrow at her retirement and their parting were preoccupied. There was one face she looked for, one voice she longed to hear telling her he loved her and wanted to marry her . . . and he wasn't here. Heart pounding with nervous tension, the strain showing on her face, she endured jolly questions about her few days off and accepted amused congratulations on her recruitment to the Seymour unit . . . but nothing could hold her attention.

At last, unable to escape completely but in an attempt to avoid Barney who was present and hopping about knocking tables over and spilling drink down strangers, Fliss backed into one of the two recesses created to provide a quiet spot for the medics to work. From there she could see most of the room. And she knew the exact moment when Nick, looking anxious and as nervous as she felt, made his entrance and swept the room with a frowning glance. But he didn't seem to see her, for he went straight to Peter and Nigel, who were standing having a joke together, and asked something. In an agony of waiting, Fliss saw them all look round; then Nigel nodded in her direction and Nick, so vital, so perplexed, was making his way towards her, ignoring attempts to engage him in conversation, his eyes only for her.

For a moment neither of them could think of a thing to say to each other. They stood together, not touching, simply drinking in the sight of the one they each thought they had lost. Fliss reached out and touched the smooth linen of his jacket with a tentative hand, and suddenly he was there with her, his arms around her waist, his sculptured features only inches from her own.

'Hold on there a moment,' said Fliss, trying to sound lighthearted though she knew the bitter test was upon her. She drew him into the depths of a nearby alcove so that they were safe from the prying eyes of half the hospital. 'You've got some explaining to do before you come any closer.' But her eyes swam with tears of sheer joy at having him close again; of profound hope that he would prove himself worthy of her trust.

'I don't have to explain anything,' he said in his deep,

stirring voice. 'But for you I will. What do you want to know? And why did you disappear so suddenly?'

'I thought . . . Well,' she began, suddenly feeling a touch of indignation with his cool attitude, 'what was I supposed to think when I walk into my best friend's flat and find you there in nothing but a bath towel? Don't start blaming me for imagining it, either. Jane's told me you left her a note, so I know it wasn't a figment of my imagination.'

'Did Jane also tell you that I'd arrived at your flat at one in the morning after spending most of the evening working on a little girl who was badly burned after drinking half a bottle of bleach?'

'The Rayner child?' asked Fliss, sidetracked. 'They found you, then?'

'Yes, they found me. What do you know about it?' he asked, puzzled.

'I was the one who did the tracheotomy on her. That's why I missed our date, you see, and why . . .'

'You mean you weren't angry because I'd stood you up?' His suspicious gaze held amusement, too. 'I thought you were so furious with me because I hadn't come round to see you when we'd arranged.'

'No, no!' Fliss's face split into a grin. 'I was late because of the child and I thought you'd got fed up with waiting and gone off to drown your sorrows with Jane.'

'When in actual fact I had to go into Bart's to help with a problem case they'd got there and was then called back to Highstead to take a look at this child . . .'

'It still doesn't explain Jane's flat,' Fliss said mischievously, anxious to hear every last word. Her fingers itched to feel the skin of his face, from the smoothness of his taut brown cheeks to the sandpaper of his chin, where already a fine dark shadow was making itself known. The top button of his shirt was undone and his tie loosened, and she knew from memory that there was a tuft of black hair just waiting to be discovered there . . .

'I meant to come round to your place, but it was nearly one by the time I finished,' growled Nick, tracing the line of her neck and shoulder with his palm, his face bent to hers as if he wanted to memorise her features. 'Your lights were out and I decided not to wake you, so I rang Jane's bell, but she wasn't in either, so I decided to take her up on her offer and use her sofa for the night.'

'She'd offered you her bed, if I understand correctly,' Fliss reminded him.

'Did she also tell you how I virtually threw it back at her?' Nick looked rueful, and Fliss wondered how she could ever have thought him to be totally uncaring and insensitive. She nodded. 'I couldn't bear to even think of you downstairs and us up there,' he murmured, and the hand that went automatically to his head to brush back his hair expressed his agitation. 'I like Jane, but I just couldn't have done it.'

Fliss could only stare. 'But we were hardly on speaking terms!' she protested at last.

'Oh, I know!' He laughed wryly. 'I didn't fall into this trap voluntarily, my darling Fliss! For a while I contemplated seducing you to strike back at your father, but after that it all backfired. No matter how much I tried to tell myself you were a scheming, cold-blooded careerist relying on your father's reputation to get you where you wanted to go, you kept proving me wrong. You didn't make a play for me; you didn't size up your prospects of a comfortable meal ticket for life; you turned out to be a good surgeon in your own right; and you showed me how . . .' He looked at the floor, then up into her eyes, and she saw that his face was filled with a gentleness and desire that made her own heart weep with longing. If he was going to find something difficult to say then she didn't want to hear it; she just wanted him to hold her, for words could never be enough.

'You showed me how a little toleration and love and understanding could make a tragedy into a blessing. When I saw you with Matt and remembered what you'd said . . .'

'But you were right! Life will be easier for him if he looks like everyone else,' Fliss cried.

'And you were right too,' he said more practically, 'so perhaps we'd better start compromising.'

'Not compromising too much, mind,' Fliss said sternly. Her mind had begun to turn again. Had she refused his proposal the other morning for the first and only time? What were his intentions now? Where did they stand?

'Now listen carefully,' Nick interrupted her thoughts. 'I'm not going to repeat this ever again, do you understand? I don't like being turned down, I warn you. But if I were to propose again, if I were to tell you I loved you and that I wanted to marry you, what would you say?'

'After a great deal of thought,' Fliss tried to look serious, though she felt like a balloon about to burst with joy and relief, 'I'd say yes. Yes, please. I love you. Marry me, Nick.'

'Oh, Fliss!' His arms caught her, held her to him so tightly that she could barely breathe. 'I've been such a shallow fool. Forgive me!'

She forgave him the best way she knew how, with kisses and murmured endearments that assured him that she felt as strongly about him as he so obviously did about her.

'Your father . . . What on earth'll he say?' Nick whispered in a moment's break from their delicious kisses.

'I dare say he'll accuse you of marrying for your own advancement,' she giggled throatily. 'After all, any man who marries Sir Mortimer's daughter is obviously only trying to cash in on her father's reputation! But seriously, Nick,' she held him away for a moment, 'there is something you may feel changes all this.'

'Nothing.'

'I've always said that if anything, God forbid, but if anything were to happen to my parents, I've promised myself that I would look after Matt. And I'll stand by that, even if I'm married. And my husband has to know and understand and agree to it.' She watched his face, so worried for a moment, relax.

'Fool! I may not be able to treat Matt quite as one should a brother-in-law, even in years to come—but you must think very badly of me to even dream I'd . . .'

'That's okay, then,' said Fliss briskly, suddenly remembering what she had in her bag.

'And with your usual efficiency you arranged the honeymoon too, you know—a good month before you knew we were going to get married. Could we fit in a fortnight in Bali before the Seymour unit is officially opened?'

Nick took the letter and read it before laughing aloud.

'Had I won the car, of course, this whole thing would be off,' Fliss joked. 'But as it's a holiday for two we might as well get married and use it as our honeymoon!'

'Very practical,' he agreed, deadpan. 'No use wasting a good opportunity, is it? Is there anything else I ought to know before I step out of this alcove and announce that we are to be man and wife?'

He raised one sexy eyebrow and stroked her hair from her face. She was no raving beauty, perhaps, but he loved her; to him she would always be beautiful because she was his wife.

'Could you work with Brian, do you think?' he asked suddenly, a cloud coming over his brow.

'Why?' asked Fliss, jolted out of her happy reverie.

'Because it may not be entirely ethical for us to work together as a team all the time. You know what people are bound to say anyway, don't you? They're going to imagine there's more than surgical skill to your appointment. But if you were to work with Brian when he comes down, as I hope he will, then they'd have to realise that you're good enough to survive on your own merits.'

'Of course I can work with him,' Fliss sighed, saddened at the realisation that she wouldn't always be working at Nick's side. But she'd have him at home, in bed at night . . . Her hands wandered over him, drawing him to her, refusing to let him go.

'I wondered if you'd care to come out of there when you've quite finished, Miss Meredith, Mr Da Costa?' Sister McIlvaney's disapproving face peeped round the corner of the alcove and her eyes opened wide. 'This is *my* party, you know, and I'm just about to be presented with my gift. And,' she softened at their glowing faces, 'people normally wait until they're married before . . .' She nodded significantly at them as they stood obliviously thigh to thigh, chest to breast.

'It's all right, Sister,' said Nick with the merest hint of laughter in his voice. 'We'll be getting married just as soon as we can.' Fliss nodded in agreement.

'Och well, *that's* all right then,' Sister beamed. 'I'll just make a wee annoucement, shall I? Meanwhile, just carry on as you were . . .'

'There'd be no stopping me,' Nick murmured tenderly as he lowered his head again to Fliss's eager lips.

'Just let her try!' his bride-to-be agreed.

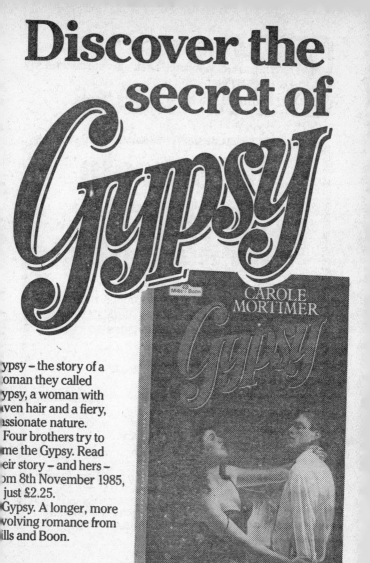

Doctor Nurse Romances

Romance in modern medical life

Read more about the lives and loves of doctors and nurses in the fascinatingly different backgrounds of contemporary medicine. These are the three Doctor Nurse romances to look out for next month.

NURSE ISOBEL'S DREAM
Hazel Fisher

LOVE'S CURE
Margaret Barker

A NURSE'S PLACE
Barbara Perkins

Buy them from your usual paperback stockist, or write to: Mills & Boon Reader Service, P.O. Box 236, Thornton Rd, Croydon, Surrey CR9 3RU, England. Readers in South Africa-write to: Mills & Boon Reader Service of Southern Africa, Private Bag X3010, Randburg, 2125.

Mills & Boon
the rose of romance